THE AIR OF MARS

And Other Stories of Time and Space

THE AIR OF MARS

And Other Stories of Time and Space

Edited and Translated by

MIRRA GINSBURG

Macmillan Publishing Co., Inc.
New York

Macmillan Publishing Co., Inc.
866 Third Avenue, New York, N.Y. 10022
Collier Macmillan Canada, Ltd.

Printed in the United States of America

1 2 3 4 5 6 7 8 9 10

Library of Congress Cataloging in Publication Data

Main entry under title:
The Air of Mars.

CONTENTS: Larionova, O. Temira.—Zhuravleva, V. The brat.—Bulychev, K. A tacan for the children of Earth. [etc.]

1. Science fiction, Russian—Translations into English. 2. Science fiction, English—Translations from Russian. [1. Science fiction. 2. Short stories] I. Ginsburg, Mirra.

PZ5.A33 [Fic] 75-34279
ISBN 0-02-736160-8

To Stephanie and Marc,
and Their Parents

CONTENTS

Editor's Note

There are no robots in this collection. Its characters are living beings, human and animal—residents of earth and of other planets, familiar and unfamiliar, present, past, and future. The stories deal with their relationships, their adventures, activities, and concerns. Some are humorous, some serious, but all are written with skill, warmth, and imagination. And all were published in the Soviet Union between 1964 and 1972.

The authors represented here are among the very best in Soviet science fiction. Most of them are scientists who are also talented writers, with a wide range of themes, interests, and styles.

In choosing the stories I sought, above all, for a fresh approach, for variety, excitement, surprise, and delight. I hope that they will give readers, both young and adult, as much pleasure as I have had in discovering and translating them.

THE AIR OF MARS

And Other Stories of Time and Space

OLGA LARIONOVA

Temira

Fevrier frowned as Boyarinov was writing out Gronning's assignment to our expedition.

"Do you have anything against him?" asked Boyarinov, his pen raised above the paper.

"N-no," said Fevrier. "But I don't care for him."

Boyarinov raised his pen still higher and stared thoughtfully at its tip. The head of an expedition had the right to bar any candidate, even without explaining his reasons.

"So you object?"

"No," repeated Fevrier.

Boyarinov shrugged and signed the paper. He relied on Fevrier, as he always did. Besides, he assumed that Gronning sooner or later would become the pride and glory of our crew.

"He still has too much of that . . . callow brashness, I guess," he said, handing the paper to Fevrier. "I'm sure you'll knock it out of him without too much trouble."

"You have a soft spot for those devil-may-care kids," said Fevrier. "What amazes me is that you've never yet made a mistake."

"And it doesn't take *you* long to put some sense into their heads," laughed Boyarinov. "One flight with a commander who doesn't make a single move without weighing it seven times over, and . . . ."

"Seven times seven," Fevrier corrected him.

"But this time I'm accepting your boy without weighing it at all."

Boyarinov threw him a quick glance, but kept silent. He felt that every word he said sounded like an apology. Though, actually, he had nothing to apologize for. He was not proposing that Fevrier take along a coward or an idler. Gronning had a brilliant record at school, an inexhaustible reserve of reckless courage, and brazen, laughing eyes.

Reggie and I had waited all this time in the corridor, and the expression on the commander's face as he came out was enough to tell us that we would, after all, be favored with the presence of that golden boy during our coming flight. Fevrier, naturally, looked as though nothing had happened.

Boyarinov was right in his own way, of course, to refuse to let us go on this trip without a trainee. The flight to Temira promised to be fairly difficult, but safe. Just the kind of flight for training novices. The system we were flying to consisted of a small, rather cool sun and three planets that held out little promise of anything important. It had been discovered quite recently, as evidenced by the designations of the planets, none of which had a mythological name. All the ancient religions had long been exhausted —they could provide no more names for the multitude of stars, planets, and large asteroids of our galaxy. And so we had before us three unknown worlds, recorded under code names and known familiarly among fliers as Temira's Planet, Atharveda's Planet, and Tanka's Wasteland. Up to now, none of our ships had landed on these planets, and we were merely a scouting group, to pave the way for a large expedition.

Accordingly, our mission was not to make any thorough

investigations; we were only to establish which planets were worth visiting, and, most important, what equipment would be needed by the main expedition.

As we had assumed, Atharveda's Planet was a smaller copy of Jupiter; Tanka's Wasteland was like an asteroid seared by cosmic cold—it did not have a trace of atmosphere; but Temira's Planet, or, as we called it for the sake of brevity, Temira, was an interesting little single-shadowed planet, with a mass approximately .75 that of Earth.

Single-shadowed planets, like our own Mercury, are always turned to their star with one side only. Such planets, as a rule, have far from optimal conditions for the development of complex organic life. Of course, their living organisms may assume utterly fantastic forms, and we expected to find them, but none of us had any hope of encountering humanoids on Temira.

The flight itself was not remarkable in any way, except for the first stirrings of initiative on Grog's part (Fevrier was the only man on board who took the trouble to pronounce our new companion's name in full). During our runs through the first six distance zones, he behaved quite decently. But as we entered the last, the seventh, and—admittedly—the most boring, performed on planetary rather than space engines, Grog began to pester the commander to make a short subspace run before shifting to planetary speeds.

Fevrier would look approvingly at his calculations with the invariable comment, "Yes, very good," but our little old *Molynel* continued to crawl on planetary speeds.

Poor Grog was ready to climb up the wall trying to convince the commander of the superiority of his method. The precision of his computations was, indeed, mind-boggling. And Fevrier would repeat, "Very good," after which he would gather up the computer cards and put them away in an empty cheese can.

"What's very good?" Grog would ask, almost crying.

"The computations."

The computations were certainly impressive. They were, in fact, quite persuasive. Nevertheless, Fevrier continued the *Molynel* on planetary speeds. He knew very well that space and time occasionally conspired together and played the most outrageous tricks on space ships. He remembered Bustamante, who came out one and a half parsecs from the calculated objective. The man made five runs, and each time erred by almost two parsecs. He was on the point of giving up flying altogether. Luckily, he didn't, for after that he never made another mistake.

No theory of probability could be applied in space—anything could happen. And did happen. It was especially bad when the ship came out into the gravitational field of some celestial body. From a planet, no matter how large, it was still possible to break away by extreme acceleration. With a star, there was only one way—to shift instantly to subspace. But this could throw the ship into such distant corners of the universe that it would be practically impossible to find the way back. Only one man, Tasaburo, had succeeded, and then by pure chance. Until the day he died, he never knew what spots in the metagalaxy his *Carmelite* had dived in and out of.

Grog may have known all this, but he was as stubborn as twenty-four donkeys, and he continued his calculations even when we had come so close to Temira that a subspace run was no longer possible. We orbited the planet along the equator and landed some fifty kilometers from the terminator line. The claws of the landing gear gripped the only bare spot of the reddish-gray Temiran soil we could discover. The rest of the land was covered by a dense, dark-olive growth. When we examined it, we found that it was a forest of small but extremely wide-spreading trees. Their branches, seemingly bare, were so closely interlaced at a height of two or three meters from the ground that they formed a solid surface that a man could walk on. The greenery was hidden beneath the branches, and no wonder: the winds on single-shadowed planets are so strong that they would instantly have torn and carried off whatever leaves might venture to appear above the tightly woven mat of branches.

The jungle beneath the crowns looked impassable—we would probably have to cut a passage through it with plasma guns.

Fevrier checked once again the firmness of the craft's grip on the landing spot and the readiness of the protective power shield. He sent out pairs of explorer robots to the sunlit and the shaded sides, and, being no pedant, allowed Reggie Scott and Gronning to come out of the ship—in light space suits, of course. I watched them through the lower viewing screen. Grog behaved quite properly this time as well, except for his repeated attempts to shake Scott's hand and congratulate him on their successful landing on the "alien saucer."

All the trainees seemed to think that calling Earth "base" and all other planets "saucers" made them sound like veterans. Fevrier detested this affectation.

I was busy at the controls, setting up all sorts of automatic stations and sending out exploring mechanisms. When I looked out again, I saw Reggie and Grog sitting on rocks, with an ugly little manikin in a masquerade costume standing before them. His clothing, made up of brightly colored patches, was stretched tightly on his puny body, like a harlequin's suit. A similarly varicolored little cap sat, by some miracle, on the tip of his head. His skinny arms and legs were in pathetic contrast to his broad shoulders and overdeveloped chest.

"Scott, Gronning, back into the ship at once!" cried the commander right at my ear.

I thought that his concern was out of place. No matter what he did now, the contact with a planetary being had already been made. But Fevrier was evidently worried that Grog might pull something foolish in a burst of enthusiasm.

The two men ran toward the ship, bending against the wind, and the manikin threw up his arms in perplexity, lost his balance and fell, but tried to crawl after the runners, taking cover from the wind behind large rocks.

We heard Reggie and Grog thump across the lock chamber. The commander and I stood at the screen: the little man still crawled toward the ship, and now we could clearly discern his sharp small face with large blue spots like bruises and purple lips, such as one sees in children with acute heart failure. The little face expressed such deep mortification and such desperate resolve that Fevrier could not resist and began to pull on his space suit.

When he went down the ladder, the manikin had already covered half the space between him and the ship. Now his expression was so darkly resolute that Fevrier could hardly doubt his bloodthirsty intentions. The commander wore a light but exceptionally strong space suit, vulnerable only, perhaps, to a medium-caliber laser, and the desintor for close combat hung at his belt, while the manikin who was advancing upon him was unarmed, half-naked, and about half his size. I had seen Fevrier in many crises, but I had never seen him so confused. I understood his state of mind; I knew he would not raise a finger against that reckless little creature, for all its aggressiveness.

Meantime, the manikin had crawled the last meter, uttered a piercing cry, and grabbed Fevrier's leg. We stood still at the screen. But the little harlequin, holding on for dear life, secured his position and rested awhile, then suddenly began to climb up the commander like a bear cub up a tree. He scrambled up to Fevrier's shoulder, peered at the human face that must have seemed enormous to him, and tapped at the front panel of the helmet, which covered the commander's face.

Fevrier did something he never would have forgiven us for had we done it—he raised the visor. The manikin was overjoyed and hurriedly began to chatter, gesticulating wildly and constantly catching at Fevrier's neck to keep from being blown off by the gusts of wind. He pointed to the edge of the platform, as though insistently inviting Fevrier to come there. Our guess was immediately confirmed in a most amusing manner. Breaking off his tirade, which seemed to me to consist of nothing but whistling, hissing, and clicking sounds (we could hear him clearly over the commander's phonotransmitter), the varicolored manikin slipped down, hurriedly unwound his belt, which turned out to be a rope of considerable length, and, before we realized it, the end of the rope was firmly knotted around the commander's leg.

All this time Fevrier maintained an air of unruffled calm, but at this point he could no longer restrain himself and burst out laughing. The little aborigine, startled at the sound, jumped aside and ran away on all fours, holding the end of the rope in his teeth. His rainbow-colored patches flashed at the edge of the wood, and he vanished, as though he had dived in.

"Reggie," said Fevrier. "I am being persistently drawn somewhere by the leg. The invitation is difficult to refuse. Look after the ship for me."

"Commander," I burst out. "What if you're being drawn into a trap?"

"A trap!" he said, a bit irritably. "Don't you see it's a child?"

And that was how man first visited the Temirans. The visit did not yield much, yet it yielded a good deal—an approximate idea of their way of life. And the life was rather odd. As Fevrier told us afterward, the Temirans lived in groups of fifteen or twenty. Each group evidently consisted of close relatives, and the family occupied one of the caves in a seemingly endless underground labyrinth that stretched along the terminator line, which divided the dark from the light half of the planet.

Their extremely low level of existence, along with traces of an unquestionably high culture, led us to suppose that the Temirans were not the original inhabitants of this scrubby planet, but had come here from somewhere else. This theory was supported by the almost total absence of animals.

Our first task now was to learn the Temiran language. Unfortunately we had only a small linguan, or linguistic analyzer, which could just barely provide approximate verbal equivalents. Besides, the Temiran language had so many unfamiliar sounds that our jaws went numb after two or three phrases. Reggie called it "twitter." But Grog showed exceptional phonetic talent; he clicked, whistled, and hissed better than all the rest of us.

Be that as it may, after a while we established some communication with the Temirans. They were, indeed, comers from another planet, which, for some reason that is still unclear to us, had ceased to exist just as they landed on Temira. It appeared that the asteroid belt we had observed between Atharveda's Planet and Tanka's Wasteland was the remains of the unlucky homeland of the present Temirans.

And then another question arose: how could the Temirans not only have survived but continued to exist for so many years under the grim conditions of a single-shadowed planet?

The Temirans explained that they succeeded only because they "warmed" each other.

This was the first time we encountered this puzzling term, which our portable analyzer could not adequately translate. Yet we had noticed that the natives were indeed treating one another with great warmth. Children were cared for by the entire family, and we saw no one giving special attention to his own child, mother, or father. In each family everyone was equally related, and everyone was addressed, gently and tenderly, as "Ayu." Strangely enough, they addressed us in the same manner. Whenever we met, the usual greeting was, "Become a member of our family," and, not knowing what the customary answer should be, we would say, simply and sincerely, "Gladly." Evidently, this was as it should be, because our entire crew very soon became, as it were, a part of every family. The Temirans treated us as close relations, and even offered us food from their less than meager stocks.

We asked our hospitable friends what they did when their reserves of dried berries (their taste was reminiscent of our figs) and cured strips of snake meat were exhausted. They told us that the entire family then went to sleep until the new crop was ripe, and their next cave neighbors who were not sleeping thought about the sleepers and warmed them.

We asked how they managed to work on their tiny berry plantations in the piercing wind, dressed only in patchwork clothes made of snakeskin. They explained that, as a rule, only half the family worked, while the rest watched and warmed them.

We also wondered how they treated their sick, and were told that families from neighboring caves gathered together and warmed the sick member back to health.

Always the same word—"warmed." The analyzer stressed that the term did not necessarily imply direct contact but was almost synonymous with our "thinking," yet with some strange connotation that still eluded us.

Grog drove himself to distraction trying to discover the precise physical meaning that our linguan failed to convey. But he might as easily have tried, with his meager supply of words, to determine how Temirans distinguished smells, which even on Earth we cannot define. A violet smells like a violet, and that's all. Besides, our hosts did not have much time for conversation. All their time was spent in the effort to secure food. Therefore Grog associated most of all with the fearless little boy who had literally "dragged" our commander to meet his family.

We called the boy Ixie. Men's names on Temira were as unpronounceable as the splendid names of the ancient Peruvians, and five or six times longer. We were obliged, shamefacedly, to use contractions, which in the beginning provoked outbursts of irrepressible merriment among the Temirans, who generally had little occasion for laughter.

We probably not only shortened, but also distorted their names, lending them amusing meanings. However, our attempts to speak their language were treated with the utmost tact, with never as much as a smile, although we must have garbled the words mercilessly.

Meantime, with the commander's permission, Grog spent his entire days with Ixie's family, taking part in their simple tasks—the weaving of baskets, the drying of berries, and the preparation of the skins of the fantastically ugly but harmless anacondas that had evolved from the experimental grass snakes released on Temira by the first settlers. Grog had a special assignment—to learn all the subtleties of the Temiran language in the shortest possible time. Naturally, he was strictly forbidden to do anything on his own without first getting the commander's permission.

We all became fond of Ixie. What at first seemed a deformity—thin legs and an enlarged chest—was characteristic of all Temirans, who had had to adapt themselves to conditions of sharply decreased gravity and a rarefied atmosphere, and we soon stopped noticing it. After several days Ixie seemed to us to be a delightful youngster, extraordinarily lively and mobile in the meager atmosphere to which even we, veteran cosmonauts who had been exposed to all sorts of conditions, did not venture to expose ourselves without a space suit or at least an oxygen mask. During his first meeting with Ixie, Fevrier had tried to walk with his visor lifted—he never did it again, and did not permit us to.

Everyone was fond of Ixie, but his devotion went entirely to Grog. The youngster became as attached to him as an earthly child might.

We had already established direct and continuous contact with Earth, and now we worked like beavers. We were showered by questions and restrictions, restrictions and questions. One day we were reminded that we were only a scouting expedition which, as everyone knows, had no right to make contact with the natives; the next day we were instructed to obtain the consent of some Temirans to be transported to Earth.

We were compiling a list of equipment and gear to be brought by the main expedition that was to follow; we tried to determine the viability of earthly plants under local conditions; we captured specimens of the local fauna—tiny, malodorous shrews and huge herbivorous anacondas whose meat tasted like smoked sturgeon; we made endless tests of the ground, the water, the air. We realized that the prime task was to help Temira produce sufficient food resources, for the greatest problem here was hunger, the curse of all backward cultures—a problem which had long since been eliminated on Earth.

Of course, the "base" could simply synthesize Temiran meat and berries, and do it so skillfully that no one would detect the difference between the artificial and the real. But to do this we first had to bring samples back to Earth, study them, and organize industrial production and delivery to Temira. These were all matters of the future—not a very distant future, but the future nevertheless, and it was not for us to solve them in detail. It troubled us, therefore, that our preliminary work proceeded so slowly. How could we enjoy our morning chocolate when we knew that a short distance from the ship little Ixie had only dried berries for his breakfast? But we knew very well that without extensive and most thorough study we had no right to offer the Temirans even a grain of salt. No wonder Fevrier repeated every morning that there must be no experiments of any kind in this respect. This, however, was meant solely for Grog's benefit—certainly not mine or Reggie's.

Our junior member, meantime, was achieving remarkable success in his linguistic studies, and supplied us every evening with new information about the Temirans. His reports were interesting, but at times rather difficult to believe. He found, for example, that the Temirans never went more than 150 or 200 meters away from their caves. Three or four neighboring caves, the tiny field cleared in the jungle, and occasional sorties into the jungle itself, but limited always to the length of the rope wrapped around his belt—this was all a Temiran knew in his lifetime. Nothing else. Descendants of cosmonauts from another planet, who carefully preserved knowledge of astronomy, physics, and mathematics, recording it on snakeskin (only leftover scraps of those skins were used for clothing) and handing it down from generation to generation, they were afraid of going more than three hundred steps from their dwellings!

It was incredible.

Next, Grog told us that our *Molynel* had landed in the field cleared by Ixie's family for planting their fig-berries. Naturally, Fevrier immediately went to see the father of our general favorite (we shortened his twenty-syllable name to Xerxes) and promised him to move the ship elsewhere. He also offered to clear a few more fields for the Temirans—this could be done with our plasma desintors in a matter of minutes. Oddly enough, Xerxes declined the offer of help.

"We wouldn't be able to use these fields, anyway," he explained with embarrassment. "They are so far from our caves that we would freeze."

Fevrier vainly argued that the temperature of the nearby

valleys was no lower than it was in his area. They simply did not seem to understand one another. When Grog said that he would continue to visit the Temirans every day even after we had moved the ship, they smiled sadly, with obvious disbelief, as though they knew we were deceiving them, but forgave the deception. And it was impossible to convince them.

Without wasting more time, Fevrier flew the ship to a new landing spot, some two kilometers from Ixie's cave. To facilitate the movement of men and jeeps from the *Molynel* to our friends' cave, we brought out the large desintor and cut a road, or rather, a tunnel, through the jungle. In our light space suits, it would be no more than a twenty-minute walk to Ixie's field. On the following day I was for some reason the only free member of the crew, and the commander permitted me to pay the first visit to Xerxes' family.

What a welcome I received! At first there was a burst of terror, then endless pitying and wailing, as if I were, to say the least, burning to death in a slow fire or being crucified in the best fashion of the ancient Romans. But gradually their grief began to give way to wonder, verging on adulation, and I finally asked Xerxes to explain what it all meant.

"We cannot understand why you are still alive," he replied with the sincerity characteristic of all Temirans.

The next day Grog set out for the cave. I had, of course, told him about the strange reception they had given me. I suggested that Temirans possibly believed in some sixth sense, something like the "psi-radiation" over which people on Earth had been puzzling for centuries without results. But Grog immediately dismissed the analogy as superficial. The extrasensory transmission of information practiced on

Earth by several arbitrarily chosen pairs of experimenters, he said, was not subject to the laws of distribution of electromagnetic vibrations; here, however, the supposed radiation was thought to depend on the distance between the source and the receptor. And this was the most likely explanation of the Temirans' fear of "freezing" when away from their relatives.

Grog concluded his argument by declaring, in his usual cocksure manner, that this belief of the Temirans was not based on any realistic biophysical phenomena, but was pure superstition. As for himself, he did not believe in any psi-fields—either here, or on Earth. And, having delivered himself of this oration, he departed.

He returned in the evening with a neat and fully formulated theory. To him, of course, it was no longer a hypothesis, but an axiom. He still denied the existence of a psi-field. However, the Temirans believed in it, and now Grog tried to convince us that this belief was the central tenet of their . . . religion. True, this religion did not assume a concrete and visible God; it was based on the assumption that a certain magical power resided in their own brains. Thus, each man's God was his own mind. In some measure, this belief was beneficial, since it helped the Temirans to survive on the new planet.

Furthermore, Grog had observed that the Temirans had no laws, no moral code, and no fixed rules of conduct. He had even asked Xerxes why no one tried to seize power, or at least to get a greater share of food—if he was stronger than the rest. Xerxes puzzled for a long time over the word "power," but it meant nothing to him. As for the distribution of their small stocks of food, he answered simply:

"None of us can do anything dishonest or unjust, because

then everybody else will think badly of him, and he will freeze."

"Completely? And only because somebody disapproves of him?"

Grog's irony was lost on Xerxes.

"Of course," he answered quietly. "It is not possible to live when everyone stops loving you. It's like . . . trying to breathe where there's no air."

"Hm," said Grog. "Then why can't a man warm himself, to use your expression?"

"No one can warm himself." Xerxes shook his head. "It's just as absurd as loving oneself. You can only warm someone else."

That was interesting, thought Grog. It turned out that the Temirans' odd superstition presupposed, first and foremost, mutual aid, and only after that, self-preservation. Naturally. When you know that everybody is ready to come to your assistance, it is easier to endure hunger and cold and underground darkness. If this were the only consequence of the Temiran superstition, it wouldn't be too bad.

On the other hand, it constantly kept the Temirans in fear of "freezing" and restricted the living space of each family to the tiny area of its cave and field. It precluded any contact between distant groups, and so prevented the development of social life and the advance of civilization. And a civilization that did not progress, argued Grog, was doomed.

Therefore, he concluded, it was our duty to make the Temirans understand the full harm of their superstitions and to prove to them in practice that there was no such thing as a psi-field.

"Just like that?" asked Reggie. "Start right off, without waiting for the expedition?"

"Why not? We can persuade one of the Temirans to put on a space suit and switch on the electromagnetic shield, and then no psi-field, even if it should exist, can penetrate inside. The Temiran will not be frightened—he'll be able to see his relatives through the transparent visor, so that the psychological factor will remain in force, but without any physical radiation."

"And you suppose, Gronning," asked Fevrier, "that the Temiran will not 'freeze' under such conditions?"

"Of course not! Ixie sat in my suit for three minutes, while I myself began to gasp for lack of oxygen. . . ."

Ixie sat in his space suit for three minutes. . . . Fevrier turned white. I don't know what another commander would have done to Grog for such a flagrant breach of rules, but ours merely went to the controls and silently tapped out in the ship's log:

"Junior pilot Gronning is not to leave the ship until special permission is granted. To be noted by entire crew."

Well, if our junior pilot had any feelings about it, he wasn't going to show them. Without a word, he signed the commander's order, sat down astride a chair, then said as if nothing had happened:

"I propose that my suggestion be discussed."

"Your suggestion will be considered when the full expedition arrives in Temira," Fevrier cut him off. "You are free, Gronning."

Grog clicked his heels and disappeared.

The next morning, at 8:00 ship's time, we all assembled for breakfast as usual. Grog asked no questions, and I knew the commander was pleased. Fevrier detested unnecessary talk. He preferred to train his men silently; the more reserved the punished man, the shorter was the punishment. I expected our prodigy to be forgiven on the very next day, but our commander decided otherwise. He left Grog to watch the ship, and we three set off for the cave village.

I don't remember what we did that whole day, but when it was time to return, Xerxes appeared next to us. He walked without a word, and we did nothing to betray our surprise.

When we reached the end of the field and entered the road cut in the thick of the Temiran jungle by our desintor, Xerxes slowed down and looked tense. It was harder for him to walk—we were in space suits, with adequate oxygen supplies, but he simply gasped in the violent wind.

Our companion fell behind, and Fevrier quickly turned to him.

"Shouldn't you go back?"

"You may be right," Xerxes agreed at once. "I've never gone so far. . . ."

I gauged the distance—it was just about 180 meters from the cave.

"Perhaps we'll walk you back?" offered Reggie Scott.

The Temiran shook his head. He stood holding onto the thick hairy lianas that hung down from the trees along the roadside, obviously trying to master himself and not succeeding.

"You don't feel well?" Fevrier asked, bending over him.

"No, no, I am simply trying to gather my strength to walk a little farther."

"You won't do that!" said Fevrier sharply. "We can't permit you to take chances."

The commander had forgotten that he was not on his

ship. Xerxes raised his face, pale enough in normal times, but now bluish from inner strain or perhaps fear, and said:

"You can forbid me to do something for you. But this is something I need—for all of us. Let us go, but a little slower, please."

We went on. With every step, Xerxes was turning a deeper purple. I walked next to him, and I saw the tiny drops of sweat that broke out on his thin neck.

"That's all," he said, stopping suddenly. "That's all. . . ."

For a while he backed away cautiously, as if afraid to take his eyes away from us. Then he turned and ran. We looked after him, and saw, by his stooping back and awkwardly flying arms, how bitterly ashamed he was to run, hopping like a rabbit over rocks and fissures in the dried soil. But there was nothing he could do; the force that was driving him toward his cave was stronger than shame or common sense.

From that day on, Xerxes went with us part of the way whenever we returned to the ship after a day's investigations. Grog was still imprisoned—I could not imagine why Fevrier was so severe this time—while we quietly accumulated information. The main expedition had already started from Earth, and we did not want to meet it empty-handed. Ixie hardly ever came up to us—he must have missed Grog. Autumn chill was gathering over the village (Temira rotated along an elliptic orbit), and we began to wonder how we could help our friends, if only for a while.

Reggie proposed lighting and warming some of the caves with a simple supply system fed by sun-powered batteries. This seemed quite practical and safe for the Temirans, and Fevrier approved the plan. The first thing to be done was to clear some land and set up solar accumulators on it. All three of us went to work. Grog was instructed to bring out the reserve lighting apparatus from the *Molynel's* hold and load it on a jeep.

We had to level the cleared platform by hand, and we worked until lunchtime. When we had finally completed the task and returned, considerably exhausted, to the ship, we found the jeep loaded to the top and Grog sitting on the step with an independent air.

If Grog had asked Fevrier, or even so much as given him a pleading look, the commander would probably have remained implacable. But Grog said nothing, and Fevrier relented.

"Take the apparatus and the batteries to the entrance of the cave, unload—and straight back. Is that clear?"

If I were in Grog's place, I'd probably have said, at least, "Yes, thanks." But Grog merely nodded. Reggie and I exchanged glances: the commander was proceeding to the second training stage—education by trust.

While our kitchen automat hissed, spat tomato juice, and stamped out traditional kebabs for lunch, we gathered in the control room near the medium phonoscreen. We could clearly see the heavy jeep roll up to the cave entrance, and its residents, alarmed by the roar of motors, coming out into the light.

I must confess that I envied Grog when I saw how Ixie welcomed him. No one had ever welcomed me like that. I imagine that was true of Fevrier as well. None of us had children, and the children of others. . . . Well, they somehow did not grow attached to us. On Earth, of course, there was never enough time—our vacations on Earth were brief. And here, all the love went to Grog.

Ixie climbed into the jeep's cabin and stayed there all the

time while Grog was unloading. Then he lay down on his stomach, with his head down, and went into a long whispered conversation with Grog. We could not hear a word over the medium phonotransmitter. And Xerxes smiled at them from the cave entrance, as though they were two children.

It was time for Grog to return. He took the boy down from the jeep and placed him carefully on the ground. Then he climbed into the spacious cabin—so spacious, you could play hide-and-seek in it. That was the thought that flashed through my mind at the moment—you could play hide-and-seek in it.

The jeep started, jerked forward, again, and again, and could not move from the spot.

"What's wrong there?" Fevrier said under his breath.

I switched on the amplifier of the helmet transmitter and repeated the commander's question to Grog.

"The motor won't start," we heard Grog's voice. "I can't imagine what's wrong with it."

I gave Fevrier a questioning glance.

"Well," he answered. "He fouled up the machine; let him fix it."

So Fevrier has pardoned him in full, I thought, and lets him stay in the Temiran village until the motor is repaired. Good for Grog.

"If you can't manage, call," I said to him, bending over the grid of the transmitter. "If you don't call, we'll come anyway after lunch."

"Good appetite," came from the jeep's cabin. Obviously, Grog wouldn't even entertain the thought that he might not manage.

Nevertheless, he did not find the cause of the breakdown

while we were eating, and after lunch we took a leisurely walk.

"Need any help?" I asked Grog when we came to the jeep.

"If I need it, I'll call you," he answered gruffly. "I'm not a baby."

I shrugged and walked toward the cave to help Reggie and Fevrier install the lights. Until now the Temirans' dwellings had been lighted by a rather fantastic method. There was a mineral on Temira that was unlike anything on Earth. After exposure to the sun, it became phosphorescent for a period of twenty to thirty hours. The gloomy caves looked otherwordly in the greenish glimmer of these light-bearing stones.

We worked until evening. Grog never approached us—apparently he made no progress with the repairs. Fevrier was, in fact, pleased: it was good practice for the young man, and a good lesson. When we passed the jeep on our way back to the *Molynel,* Grog pretended he did not see us. The collar of his space suit was open, his sleeves were rolled up above the elbows, his helmet was off, and only the white tube of the oxygen-supply apparatus quivered at his lips.

Fevrier smiled, but said nothing. I knew our commander, and thought, heaven help our junior pilot if he fails to repair the jeep now. Xerxes walked along with us. As usual. But before we had covered eighty meters, he suddenly slowed up. His face assumed the characteristic purplish hue, his hands would not obey him and caught at every liana. He was like a child who clutches at his mother's skirt as he listens to a frightening story.

Ten steps more, and he stopped.

"I can't," he muttered. "Today I can't. . . ."

He raised his face—the pitiful face of a midget—and

looked at us guiltily, as the weak might look at the strong when the latter had done something unjust or cruel.

It was all very strange.

He looked at Fevrier, then at me, then at Reggie, then back at the jeep we had left behind, and finally, opening his blackened lips with an effort, whispered reproachfully:

"It wasn't right. . . ."

We did not understand him, but he was already running, flopping his arms absurdly, as he had the first time.

And Grog, wiping his hands with a rag, watched him with an odd expression from the step of the jeep.

We went on slowly, and I couldn't for the life of me understand what had frightened our companion so much, and why he was reproachful.

When we reached the ship, Fevrier halted, letting us get in first. He was visibly worried by something. I walked up several steps, then I turned and asked:

"What 'wasn't right'?"

" 'It wasn't right to think so badly of us'—that's what," answered Fevrier. "They've learned, after all, to receive that blasted 'psi-warmth' from us as well. That's what made it possible for Xerxes to walk farther and farther from his cave with us every day. We warmed him. Like his own family. But today he felt that someone was unfriendly to him."

I recalled Grog, slowly wiping his hands on the step of the jeep. What were the words he brought us from the cave about a week ago? Involuntarily, I spoke the words aloud:

"If people think badly of someone, he will freeze. . . ."

"Yes," said Fevrier, who seemed to be thinking of the same thing. "The cold of indifference, of distrust, of hostility or contempt. We read about it in fiction, and take it as a figure of speech. But they freeze."

I glanced at him with astonishment. So he believed it! He evidently believed all that nonsense about "psi-warmth" from the very first. . . .

"All right." Fevrier waved his hand. "That will do for today. I'll get him back now."

I quickly ran up the steps and went to the panel. Fevrier would now order the junior pilot to quit work and return to the ship. A pity. The young man could have shown his mettle. . . . But what had he been thinking of, watching us walking away with Xerxes? However, it was easy enough to guess: he got hell for an innocent experiment with the space suit, but Fevrier himself was calmly experimenting, leading that wretched little Temiran away from the source of his "psi-field." Incautious, and damned unfair!

Then suddenly on the screen I caught sight of the jeep, moving along the edge of the field. Slowly at first, then in jerks, as if trying different speeds. On, and on.

"Commander!" I cried. "Our *wunderkind* has done it!"

Fevrier nodded dryly.

The jeep crawled like a cautious turtle into the narrow entrance of the road, and, reassured, we went about our own tasks. Twenty minutes later we heard the clatter outside as the jeep was rolling into the cabin of the elevator. I switched on the sound to congratulate Grog, but at that moment we heard a breaking, unrecognizable voice:

". . . dare to freeze! Don't dare! Get up, I tell you!"

It was Grog's voice.

Fevrier, who, like the rest of us, had already taken off his space suit, dashed to the hatch, then to the control panel, but the voice fell silent. We heard only the sound of whistling, broken, heavy breathing. Suddenly the air was filled with a spray of sounds—something creaked, clanked, and grated, as though trying to tear its way out of a metal maw, and at the same moment we saw on the screen and through the porthole how the jeep dropped out of the elevator and sped away from the ship.

"Halt!" Fevrier shouted hoarsely. "I order you to halt!"

The communication system worked—we clearly heard Grog's breathing and the roar of the motors.

"Stop the jeep!"

No answer.

The jeep disappeared from the field of direct vision, but on the viewing screen its hulk loomed clearly, and we saw it lurching from side to side—Grog's hands would not obey him.

Somewhere halfway the motors screeched and fell silent. The dark hulk on the screen jerked and stopped dead.

"Crashed, the son of a. . . ." said Reggie. We could see it ourselves. "Burn it!" Reggie cried into the microphone. "Cut the damned trees with the plasma gun, idiot!"

Grog evidently did not hear us. The connection was on, but he was simply incapable of grasping anything. Besides, it would have done no good to cut the trees with the desintor—the motor was as dead as it had been earlier.

Grog must have realized it, because we saw on the screen a little spot separating itself from the jeep and slowly moving on. Slowly. That meant that Grog was carrying something.

Without a word, we rushed to the hatch. No one put on his space suit—there was no time. This was an unheard-of breach of rules, as was the fact that all of us were leaving the ship, with no one staying on duty. It would have made no sense to try to get the reserve jeep out of the *Molynel's* hold—this would have taken at least an hour.

We ran at the maximum speed possible to well-trained men in that rarefied air, which meant that we were barely moving. Without a glance we hurried past the jeep, tangled in the greenery. It was essential to catch up with Grog. We never did. He, after all, was in his space suit.

When at long last we reached the field, Grog had already entered the cave. We were no longer running. We dragged ourselves along, gasping for air, in which, it seemed to me, there wasn't an atom of oxygen. I glanced at Reggie—he was blue. Fevrier walked ahead, and I could not see his face. The only thing that saved us was that the wind was from behind.

We managed to get to the cave. My only thought was: lucky that Grog was in his suit, or he never would have made it with his burden.

But what was the good of it?

At the very entrance to the cave I lost my breath, and was the last to crawl inside. Everyone was standing—Ixie's family, Fevrier, Reggie, and that scoundrel, Grog. They stood without motion, and such an anguished silence filled the cave that I could not, dared not, move beyond the entrance.

After a moment, my eyes became accustomed to the glimmering light of the phosphorescent stones, and I realized that they were standing over Ixie's body. And he lay there, in his motley suit, like a little tightrope dancer at a village fair who had lost his footing.

Fevrier recovered himself first. I thought with horror that he would try to speak, to explain. But he merely bowed his head to Xerxes. Then he turned sharply, went to the doorway, and stood aside, as if to let someone pass. He did not even glance at Grog, but Grog understood and slowly walked out between me and Fevrier.

We followed.

Grog walked back to the ship. He walked rapidly—of course, he was in his space suit. Again, we could not keep up. When we got aboard, he was already in his cabin.

Fevrier went straight to the controls and switched on the starter engines. According to emergency rules, I had to check whether the locks were airtight, but I could not believe that we would go without even trying to save the child with our powerful medicine and technology.

The commander threw me a questioning glance.

"What about the quantum reanimator?" I muttered.

Fevrier shook his head.

"Too late. It's more than forty minutes. Besides, we have no idea of their anatomy. . . ."

"Yes," said Reggie. "Forty minutes is too late. You can believe me. I was on Nii-Naa, searching for Abakumova's group. Everyone was frozen. We didn't manage to save any of them."

"But still, freezing is only an analogy," Fevrier spoke wearily. "This is something much more terrible. The organism gives up at once and irreversibly. And without any visible causes. . . ."

The causes will never be visible to us.

Of course, it's bad to be without friends or loved ones who think about you constantly, and, most important of all, with endless good will. One feels lonely and depressed. But dying from it? That is beyond human understanding. We knew how strongly the Temirans believed in it, but now Ixie had died of it before our very eyes—and yet our minds could not accept it.

The child had frozen even before the jeep approached the ship. He froze at once, as soon as he remained alone with that son of a bitch, who was incapable of any emotion except cold curiosity. And surely curiosity could never warm anyone. . . .

"Start!" the commander ordered.

The outside sirens barked. According to rules, we had to inform Grog about the start and wait till he, like every other member of the crew, reported himself ready before the engines were switched on. But Fevrier merely pressed the internal signal button, and that was all.

We lifted off.

For two hours or so we flew on planetary motors, swinging away from Temira. Then the cosmic generators went to work and the automatic pilot rocked the ship, setting the course for Earth. The commander sat with lowered head. He waited for contact with the caravan of ships that should by now be approaching the system of Temira. He waved his hand, and we retired to our cabins. To sleep? As if a man could sleep after what had happened that evening.

Of course, it was foolish to blame Grog alone. But that night we could not see it any other way. I suppose it was worse for him than for all of us taken together, but we could not feel sorry for him. We cursed him, and the day when he had been assigned to the *Molynel,* and the hour when he stepped on Temiran soil.

Yet it must really have been bad for him that night. In two weeks the ship would land, and then—then something awaited him much more terrible than our hate or our contempt. As far as the *Molynel* was concerned, he could simply leave it. He could even retire from the cosmic fleet.

But he would, anyway, remain the junior pilot Gronning, whose duty it was to report at Lanka and declare himself a murderer before the Council for the Investigation of Extraordinary Acts.

In the past, people accused others. Today a man can only accuse himself. This is immeasurably more difficult.

Dozens of people would defend him from his own conscience. No one would accuse him—this was not done anymore. Everybody would look for extenuating circumstances, but what if they could not be found?

And then he would be left for life with the charge of murder, ancient as the world itself—a terrible charge that he had not been cleared of.

Perhaps the murder was accidental? Ixie, nimble as a squirrel, might easily have slipped into the jeep's cabin, so spacious that one could play hide-and-seek in it, and concealed himself in order to repeat the experiment his father had attempted every day. Grog truly might have failed to notice the boy, but does not involuntary murder result in death as final as deliberate murder?

At six in the morning we came to the control room, first I, then Reggie. Fevrier had never left it. There was still no contact with the expedition; the report on what had happened still lay near the long-distance panel.

The commander looked at us.

"I shall make my report now," he said in an even voice. "I would like the entire crew to be present."

Of course, it was cruel to force Grog to listen to the communication, but I felt nothing except "It serves you right, you bastard."

Fevrier clicked on the intercom switch.

"Gronning, report to the control room!"

The usual "Yes, sir" did not follow.

The ship's system ordinarily conveyed every sound from the cabins. We expected to hear the creaking of the cot and the sound of the sliding door opening.

Grog's cabin was silent.

Fevrier repeated his order. Again, without result. He glanced at Reggie questioningly, and Reggie left the room. We heard him slide open the partition, heard his step in the cabin, then silence. Finally, he spoke:

"Come here, commander. He is frozen."

I had also seen frozen people—not on the Nii-Naa asteroid, but on the Twenty-Sixth accident buoy. I knew what it meant. We stood over Gronning's cot, and it did not take us long to realize we could do nothing. Everything was over hours ago. He was lying face up, as calm as a man who had thrown off a heavy burden. And we knew that we would find no visible causes to explain why his life had stopped.

"A man cannot live if everyone around thinks badly of him," said Fevrier quietly, and neither of us dared to say that this was true only for the natives of Temira.

We looked at Grog's calm face and felt more and more the burden of our guilt. Whatever he had done, we killed him.

In conclusion, let me say that we were exonerated on Lanka. But that meant nothing to us, because we were tried only by men. If there had been any Temirans on the Council, they surely would have found us guilty.

And this, properly speaking, is the whole story of our first expedition to Temira's planet.

VALENTINA ZHURAVLEVA

THE BRAT

I first saw her three years ago. At that time she was the quietest little girl. She timidly asked for autographs and stared at writers with eyes round with wonder.

In the course of three years she never missed a single meeting of the Association of Science Fiction Writers. Actually, no one invited her. But no one chased her out, either. She sat on the edge of a chair and avidly drank in every word. She listened with rapt attention, even to those who mumbled the most boring nonsense.

We gradually became accustomed to her. We became accustomed to her silence. And when she finally began to speak, she took us all by surprise. This happened during a discussion of a new novel, wishy-washy and overburdened with popular-scientific commentary. The author was extremely pleased with his work, and our critical remarks made no impression on him whatsoever.

"Let's see now," he said with a benign smile, "why don't we ask the child. 'Out of the mouths of babes,' as the saying goes. Hm. . . . Well, then, my dear child, was there anything you liked in my book?"

The "dear child" answered readily:

"Oh, yes."

"Excellent, excellent!" said the author and, smiling encouragingly, he asked: "And what, exactly?"

"Antokolsky's poem. Eight lines on page fourteen—really something!"

I suddenly realized that the little girl, round-eyed with wonder, was no longer there. Instead, there was an impudent brat in green slacks and a lilac leather jacket, its pockets bulging with books. And eyes with a wicked glint in them, outlined (not yet too skillfully) with a dark pencil.

From that moment on our meetings turned, to quote the first victim, into "smoking sessions near an open box of dynamite."

I was treated by the Brat with a certain tolerant condescension. She saved her most caustic comments for my ears, as she walked me home. One day I invited her in, and after that she came almost every evening. She did not disturb me too much. She rummaged through my books, and whenever she found something that interested her, she'd settle down with it silently for hours on my sofa. Of course, her silence was only relative. She gnawed at her nails, snorted approvingly, and whistled at passages that especially pleased her. According to her, that was how the lobsterspiders whistled in some story she had read. She read everything, not only science fiction.

"Incidentally," she announced, putting aside a small volume of Shakespeare, "Romeo was a fool. I'll tell you how he should have stolen Juliet. . . ."

But her real love was science fiction. She read even the dullest stories, from the first word to the last, then stared at the ceiling for a long time with unseeing eyes. She set herself in the hero's place, reshuffled the plot, and quickly lost all distinction between what she had read and what she was inventing.

Once, for example, she declared in all seriousness that she had met an invisible cat.

"The sound was there, but the cat couldn't be seen. I knew immediately it must be the one."

"Which one?"

"The cat in Griffin's experiment. Don't you remember? Kemp asked the Invisible Man, 'You don't mean to say there's an invisible cat at large?' And Griffin said, 'Why not?' Oh, how could you forget such things? And the invisible cat must have invisible kittens, too. Just imagine!"

Generally, the Brat noticed details in science fiction that people seldom pay attention to. What, she would ask, has become of the model of the time machine? The model, not the machine itself. Wells says in passing that the model went off traveling in time. Many people after Wells wrote stories about time machines. How come there's not a single story about that traveling model?

She was most interested, however, in the still-unsolved problems of science. "Why not now?" became her favorite question. She pronounced it as a single word, "Whyn'tnow?" For example, is it possible to revive the severed head of some professor? "And whyn'tnow?" Is it possible to fill the bathtub with liquid helium and stick somebody in for anabiosis? "Whyn'tnow?"

One day she chanced upon a story about man's flight on wings equipped with "electroplastic" muscles. For a long time she turned the magazine this way and that, studying the illustrations. Then she asked, "Whyn'tnow?"

She stopped reading and nearly drove me out of my mind for three days with her "whyn'tnow." Finally, I took her to a friend of mine, an engineer. He was a man of astounding patience—he could converse for hours even with inventors of perpetual-motion machines.

The Brat immediately presented the magazine with the story and began an endless series of her "whyn'tnows." The engineer took down some books on the theory of flight and gave her a detailed explanation of "why not now."

The larger the living creature, the less favorable the correlation between the power at its disposal and its weight. This is why, he said, large birds like white swans don't fly well. A horse couldn't fly even if it had wings. Man's weight is somewhere on the borderline: the power he can supply is sufficient to raise about 150 to 170 pounds into the air. But the weight of the wings must also be taken into account, and then the correlation becomes unfavorable.

The engineer explained all this to the Brat with the utmost care, citing figures, graphs, and examples. She listened without interrupting him, but wrinkled her nose contemptuously. I did not know her well enough as yet to realize what this meant.

For about ten days after that the Brat stayed away. Then she came with a shabby valise, tied together with a rope. I thought she was going away somewhere.

"I've got wings here!" she burst out.

She simply jumped with impatience. I was amazed that the Brat had actually made something. Up to now she had confined herself to theoretical discussions.

"The boys made them." She spoke slowly, even solemnly, in contrast to her usual manner. "I thought them up, and they made them."

This was something new: the Brat had boys now.

"I'll explain it right away," she said, tugging at the rope

which held the valise together. "We've tried them already—they work!"

I was accustomed to her notions and expected to hear something fantastic. But she developed her idea, which was, indeed, simple, clear, and, in any case, credible. She explained everything briefly, in a few words.

Man weighs too much to fly on wings; hence there is no sense in building muscle-planes. This fact was tackled by the Brat in her own way. The conclusion: muscle-planes should be built for animals, which are lighter than man.

"Anyway, it is pure egotism," she declared. "Why has man, for thousands of years, been thinking of wings only for himself? Why not make wings for animals?"

Indeed, why not? This turn of thought was unexpected, and I did not know how to answer it.

The battered valise contained a large red tomcat. He lay on an umbrella, or, to be more precise, on a former umbrella, for now it was a pair of wings.

"You'll see, right away," said the Brat as she began to put the wings on the tom.

The tom submitted with absolute calm. I had never seen such a marvelously imperturbable cat. He made no protest of any kind as the Brat attached the wings to his body with leather straps. With the wide black wings, the tom resembled a pterodactyl in an illustration for a science fiction novel. But I repeat, he was an incredibly phlegmatic tom. He wasn't in the least impressed by the fact that he was the first winged cat in the world. Squinting lazily, he looked around the room, wagged his fluffy tail with utmost good humor, and ambled toward the armchair. The wings, attached to his paws with rubber bands, dragged after him, rustling on the floor. After a moment's thought, the tom climbed into the chair, gathered the wings under him, curled up, and instantly fell asleep.

I explained to the Brat where she had miscalculated. "It isn't enough to have wings," I said. "The entire organism must be adapted to flight—and not only the body, but also the psyche. Ability to fly is not enough; there must also be the impulse to fly."

My argument was very logical, but the Brat wrinkled her nose and shook her head.

"Imagine, psyche!" she said contemptuously. "He's got a psyche, too!"

She brought her jacket from the foyer, rummaged in its vast pockets, and put a mouse on the table. A real, live mouse.

The rest happened in a fraction of a second.

The red tom leaped with lightning speed, as if he had been shot out of a cannon. He probably calculated his leap with absolute precision, but he forgot his wings. They opened with a swishing noise when he was already in the air. And the tom flew clear across the table. It was a giant leap; if not for the wall, he probably would have flown at least forty yards. But he crashed into the wall, shook his head in a daze, and soared up to the ceiling. The wings creaked and flapped, terrifying the tom, and he tossed madly back and forth around the chandelier. Then something must have happened to the wings. The tom turned a somersault, and tumbled, hissing, back into the chair.

For a while we were silent; nothing was heard except the tom's heavy breathing.

"Too bad," the Brat said finally. "I should have brought a bat, not a mouse. He would have caught it easily. What do you think, does our national economy need flying toms?"

I hastened to assure her that the national economy would get along perfectly well without flying toms. And without flying dogs. I mentioned dogs because I was sure the Brat would think of them next.

"Flying dogs?" she repeated pensively. "They'd be fine to watch over herds and flocks. But, then, it would be better if those . . . whatd'you call 'em . . . could fly themselves. Then it wouldn't be necessary to watch them."

"Whom?"

"Oh, the sheep," the Brat said impatiently. "The sheep. . . . They'd fly up to the mountain pastures—wouldn't that be something?"

At this point I realized that it was necessary to be extremely careful with her; she might turn any idea in some unexpected direction of her own, and no one could tell what it would lead to. Choosing my words with care, I explained to the Brat that it was not by chance that some animals had wings and others didn't.

She silently packed the tom in her valise.

"Don't worry about it," I said as she was putting on her leather jacket. She glanced at me with absent eyes and answered vaguely:

"Of course. . . ."

A week later the local newspaper carried an item, "Can Hens Fly?" The author, a student of the biological sciences, wrote that many of the town residents had observed a remarkable natural phenomenon—a hen that flew at a great height for a long time. Until then, wrote the scientist, everyone assumed that hens' wings were poorly adapted for flight, but evidently man had not yet learned all there was to know even about so seemingly familiar a creature as the hen. The item concluded with the following words: "In time, science will unquestionably solve this riddle of nature as well."

I did not doubt for a moment that there was no riddle of nature to be solved here, but that the Brat must be behind it all. I myself had told her that wings must not be a useless burden. And this may have led her to the thought of useless chicken wings.

I telephoned the engineer I had visited with the Brat.

"You know, there is something to it," he said after listening to my jumbled account. "No, I mean it. After all, take the science of bionics: technology copies nature. Why shouldn't there be a science of the reverse? The girl may be regarded as the founder of a new science, devoted to grafting technology onto nature. Take horses, for example: don't we shoe them? . . . Flying sheep, eh? I don't know, I don't know, but if you consider a hare or a jerboa. . . . One moment, I'll make a rough calculation. . . ."

The next day the paper carried a new item, this time in the section of "Curious Events." The item noted sadly that the swans, which had lived and prospered for eight years in the ponds of the city park, had suddenly risen into the air and taken off at enormous speed to parts unknown.

I was rereading the item when my doorbell rang. It was the Brat. I had never seen her in such high spirits.

"I have a brilliant idea!" she announced from the threshold. She was exceedingly pleased with herself and in no way disturbed by my gloomy looks. "I'll tell you all about it. . . ."

"Concerning hens?" I asked.

"Oh, hens—that's nonsense!" The Brat waved me off. "Imagine, hens. . . ."

Then I asked about the swans. She wrinkled her face impatiently.

"The swans are nonsense too. Perhaps they decided to spend most of their time in the air. . . . We only lengthened their wings. We glued on more feathers. So the wings wouldn't be a useless burden. You know, even pigeons' wings could be extended. For speed. But fish are much more interesting."

"Fish?" I repeated, to gain time.

"Yes. You know, their fins are also like wings. Let's take a dolphin: can you imagine how marvelously it could fly? Or a swordfish. . . . Even now it can swim a hundred miles an hour. And if you attach wings. . . . But tell me, does the national economy need flying fish?"

For a moment I was stunned. I simply didn't know how to answer her. The brazen kid before me suddenly appeared to me as the very incarnation of fantasy—as fantasy itself. The incarnation was impatient, it refused to bow to any obstacles, it stood there with scratches on its nose and sharp glints in its eyes. Something had to be done, and I reminded her of evolution: wings and fins, I said, are the result of a long process of selection, leading to the most efficient forms required by the given organism.

"Imagine, evolution!" the Brat interrupted me. "Well, evolution isn't finished, is it? It goes on, but slowly. Why should we wait for the future? Whyn'tnow? Everything can be done faster. I mean, speed it up, this evolution. . . ."

I had an alarming vision of her "speeded-up" world, in which flying cats pursued bats, winged dogs pursued winged dolphins, and fishermen attached their nets to balloons floating in the sky to catch flying fish. The thought flashed through my mind that I had released a jinn from a bottle. I felt—quite seriously!—my responsibility before mankind.

Then came a saving thought. It was a lucky thought and, what's more, it came at the right moment. Another delay, and nothing could have stopped the Brat.

"Imagine, wings!" I said, carefully imitating her intonations. "Anybody can fly on wings. After all, it's old-fashioned by now to fly on wings. But if you take antigravitation—that's something else. Of course, some people feel that it's a matter for the distant future. But why? Whyn'tnow?"

And now, as I write these words, the Brat sits by the window in my armchair, her feet curled under her. She is reading *Physics for Everybody.* For the past two months she has been reading nothing but physics. No extraordinary events have taken place during these months. She sits with her nose buried in the book, chewing her nails and mechanically twisting her hair around her finger. Everything is quiet and peaceful.

Quiet and peaceful. For the time being.

KIRILL BULYCHEV

A Tacan for the Children of Earth

The tacan was captured at the edge of the Great Plateau, where the trackless gray jungle gives way to scattered groves of purple trees that spread around them the acrid smell of camphor and ether. The purple trees have long, poisonous needles, and if a careless traveler stops for the night in a grove, he will never awaken. The gray mists never reach the plateau, and the snow-capped summits of the Cloud Range are visible in all weather.

The tacan was captured by Cana hunters and brought to the village near the waterfall. He was still too young to fly. The hunters did not kill him because the chief of the Darka post had visited the village that winter and said that a live tacan could be sold for a large sum of money.

The wound on the animal's shoulder was soon healed, but he did not run away into the mountains. He was less than a year old, and he grazed in the meadow with the longlegs and returned with them in the evenings. The elder's daughter brought him salt and saw to it that the longlegs didn't hurt him. The elder harnessed a jumping worm and went to Darka, to tell the chief of the post that the hunters had caught a tacan and now expected a large sum of money for it. The chief sent a message to the capital, and that was how I learned about it. The elder went back to his village. Before he left, he swore by the spirits of the mountains that the tacan would remain safe and sound.

This was the first tacan ever captured alive. Ten years earlier, the botanist Gulayev, who was studying the plants of the Great Plateau, had seen the skin of an unknown animal in the cave temple of the worshipers of the Blue Sun. The skin was old and worn, with bare spots in its thick, golden fur. The head priest of the temple sat on it. Gulayev was interested in the Ox orchid, an ordinary looking plant with small five-petaled flowers, whose roots contained paulin. Paulin makes it possible for a man to go without sleep for as long as a month without any ill effect. The worshipers of the Blue Sun were known for their long vigils, and the people in Darka had advised Gulayev to speak to the head priest. The priest pretended that he did not know anything about the orchid, but he told the visitor from Earth that the animal whose skin had attracted his attention lived high in the mountains and could not be captured alive. The animal's name was tacan, and it was guarded by the evil spirits of the mountains. After that the priest said something to his attendant, who brought in something thin and transparent like a piece of mica and said that it came from a tacan's wing. The tacans fly during the summer season, and in the fall they shed their wings. Gulayev forgot all about the orchid and offered a high price for the skin and the piece of wing. The high priest refused to part with them, but allowed them to be photographed.

I had seen a three-dimensional photograph of the skin and wing when I was still on Earth. Gulayev had brought it to the zoo.

On Zea, I gathered a fine collection of animals. I had an especially large number of jumping worms, and people in the museum assured me that they would acclimate themselves easily on Earth and that they were invaluable as beasts of burden and could also be used for riding. Still, I had an odd repugnance to the idea of riding a worm, and I suspected that my fellow Earthmen would share this prejudice.

I learned all that could be learned about tacans, which was very little. No museum and no zoo on the planet had any examples, and many zoologists simply dismissed them as a fiction. They helped me, however, to send messages to the mountain regions, promising a generous reward for the capture of a tacan. And two months later came the news that a young tacan had indeed been captured. It was extraordinary luck.

The chief of the Darka post escorted me to the village. The elder came to the boundary fence to welcome us. His four arms were adorned with stone bracelets. He was followed by hunters with short spears.

During his month's stay in the village, the tacan had grown to the size of the longlegs. He recognized the elder and came when he called. Raising his head, he looked at us with his large golden eyes. He was very charming, and I felt sorry that the Zeans didn't know our legend. So the Winged Horse did exist—sixteen parsecs from Earth!

I put out my hand to stroke him, and the elder said:

"He's good."

The elder was very anxious for me to like the tacan.

We spent the night in the village. At night I found it difficult to breathe and woke up. I opened my valise to get the oxygen mask. While I was puttering with it, I lost all desire to sleep and went out into the street. At the end of the street was the enclosure for the cattle, and I caught sight of the tacan. He was not sleeping either. He stood leaning on the fence and looked at the blue mountains, just touched by the dawn. His fur was faintly phosphorescent. He heard my steps and turned his head. I stopped, overcome by the certainty that the tacan was about to speak to me. But he was silent. I was suddenly ashamed because I had deprived him of his mountains, because I was planning to put him into a cramped space ship and take him to Earth. But I tried to shake off the feeling. After all, animals lived longer in zoos than in freedom.

"Sleep," I said to him. "We have a long journey before us. People are waiting for you."

The tacan sighed and shifted from foot to foot.

We paid the elder a thousand, exactly what he asked. Another four thousand had to be paid to the Darka officials. The elder regretted asking so little. He had said "a thousand," never thinking that there were beings capable of paying so much for a tacan.

The tacan could not be brought to Darka on the same day—our jeep was too small. The others left, and I remained in the village to wait for a larger vehicle. I had a movie camera and I spent hours photographing the tacan, the urchins who followed me wherever I turned, and old Sopa. The old man had two more arms than the other hunters of his tribe, and he looked like an Indian god. He sat on the doorstep of his hut and squinted indifferently at my camera with his three eyes. I was glad I remained in the village. Over it loomed the bluish-gray mountains, and on the village square, under a pine, stood a wooden idol smeared with grease. One of his wings was cracked and tied in place with a dirty rope.

I tired quickly, but used little oxygen. At night I was tormented by nightmares: I dreamt that the tacan had escaped to the mountains, and I climbed after him through the poisonous needles, trying to catch up with him in the snowy passes, and forever falling behind. My eyes hurt from the gleaming of his fur. Then he flew up to the clouds, and his dragonfly wings looked like a whiff of grayish mist in the sky.

The hunters took me with them to the woods to look for snakes. The woods were filled with autumnal stillness. There had been no rain for many weeks. Dry grasses rustled underfoot. I gathered a bunch of small pink flowers. They smelled of mold and their petals were moist to the touch. I wanted to dry them as a souvenir, but by evening they melted away.

Two days later a large truck came, with a cage. Its motor, struggling with the steep ascent, could be heard half an hour before it appeared. I wanted very much to remain in the village and hoped the motor would break down. I wanted to see the gray-blue mountains every morning. But I went to the tacan, to look him over before departure. The elder's daughter, who disliked me because I was taking away the tacan, came out to say good-by to him, and waved as the truck was turning behind the last hut. The cage swayed on the turns, and the tacan quickly shifted from foot to foot to keep his balance.

In the plane he stood with his warm head on my knees, and his eyes were sad. He moved his lips, as though trying to whisper something to me, and I reassured him and scratched his steep forehead.

At the capital's airport we were met by an unexpected crowd—high officials, cosmonauts from other planets, and the curious. The first to approach the plane was the director of the local zoo. He was impatient to see the tacan. He would have preferred to keep him, but the Darka officials had sold the animal to Earth, and the central government did not interfere. The government wanted the tacan to be a present to Earth. Now that all doubts of his reality were dispelled, the Zeans hoped to get a few more for themselves.

I led the tacan down the gangway to the plastic-paved airfield, and everybody tried to come close to him and stroke his warm, silky flank. The tacan waited patiently until he could get away somewhere into the shade. He felt hot in the valley, and his sides rose and fell heavily as he breathed the sultry air.

He was placed in an air-conditioned room in the cosmic service building. We wanted him to acclimate himself and get stronger before the journey to Earth.

The tacan was unhappy. He refused the unfamiliar grass. Every day I argued with the chemists who were trying unsuccessfully to find suitable food for the captive. In the evenings crowds of visitors gathered outside the room, but I tried to keep them out. I became very fond of the tacan. It seemed to me that he was also dreaming of gray-blue mountains and distant snowy clouds.

It was hot in the capital. By morning the scattered, delicate clouds melted away and gray dust hung in the air outside the window. I worked in the tacan's room, which was cooler. From time to time he got up from the wilted grass spread for him on the floor, approached me from behind, and, trying not to disturb me, watched me as I typed.

The ship from Earth was late. I sent home message after message describing the critical condition of my valuable animals, to no avail. I collected the receipts for the messages and waited for Saturday, when I visited our embassy and received from the perspiring, irritable accountant local money for the maintenance of the animals and of myself. The accountant was mortally afraid of the jumping worms and tried to stay indoors lest one of them jump on him. I invited him to come and take a look at the tacan, but he merely waved his hand: he had long put childish fairy tales behind him.

Often, in the evening, the tacan and I held long conversations. To be exact, I talked, and he agreed. Or did not agree.

"Look," I said, "we must bring people joy. That is our task—yours and mine."

The tacan bent his head sideways, to his shoulder. He was thinking. His lashes, long and straight as swords, crossed whenever he narrowed his eyes.

"And children," I said, "must believe in legends. They are waiting for you because you are a legend. Come to Earth with me. I beg you."

"I will," he answered one evening. His first wings were just growing out. They itched, and he scraped the walls of the room with their sharp edges.

"All the television channels will announce your coming. And everyone will gather to meet you."

The tacan put his warm, heavy head on my knees.

"You'll like our grass. It is just like the grass on your mountains."

The city was suffocating in the fiery mists. They interfered with breathing. The director of the zoo came to visit us. He drank terrestrial lemonade and spoke about his problems at the zoo, the diseases of carnivorous plants, and the breeding habits of three-headed snakes. I listened absentmindedly, thinking that I would have to move the tacan to the zoo. For the time being.

I sent two more "lightning" messages to Earth. The embassy called to say that the passenger liner *Orion* had altered its course to pick us up. The liner would take at least two weeks to reach the capital.

A letter came from the elder's daughter. It was written for her by the letter-writer in the Darka marketplace. The girl said that her father had divided a hundred among the hunters who had captured the tacan and had deposited nine hundred in the bank in Darka. The old man knew the value of money. Each hunter got twenty pieces and gambled them away at once in the marketplace. The elder's daughter also wrote that the hunters found tracks of adult tacans, but the animals themselves were gone—they had flown away.

I wrote the girl that the tacan was doing well, and would do still better when the Earth ship came for us. I told her not to worry, because I took good care of him.

We transferred him to the zoo. He had become very weak and walked with difficulty to the cluster of green trees in the center of the enclosure where the hairy birds lived. The birds were not troubled by the heat; their normal habitat was in the hot volcanic swamps. At the entrance to the zoo, the director put up a sign saying that the only tacan ever captured alive was on exhibit there before departure for Earth.

In addition to the trees, there was a little swamp with heated water inside the enclosure. The hairy birds busily poked about in the mud. From time to time a three-armed fish leaped out of the water. The birds fought and squawked loudly.

Visitors came to the zoo in families, leaving their worms at the gate. They brought small rugs and saucepans with them. They stared at the golden animal in the shade of the trees, but they were more interested in the hairy birds, because the Earth and Zea had altogether different legends. The main heroes of the Zean legends were fiery serpents and hairy birds.

After lunch on the grass, the visitors went to see the singing snakes, which were constantly in motion and were completely unmusical. The snakes imitated the visitors, who tried to guess what they were doing and laughed. Sometimes boys threw pebbles at the tacan to make him get up and come to the railing. They teased him and called him "longlegs." The tacan did not get up. When I came to him, he sighed and attempted to raise his wings, almost invisible in the shade. At those times large crowds gathered at the railing, for I was a greater marvel to them than the tacan. The boys seemed to think that I was also an exotic animal because I had only two arms and two eyes, but they did not throw pebbles at me.

The telephone rang in my room at three in the morning. The director of the zoo told me, stuttering with anxiety, that the tacan was very sick. I cried into the receiver that I was coming right over. I switched on the table lamp and struggled to get into my shirt—my hands seemed unable to find the sleeves.

The tacan had gotten worse in the evening, before the zoo closed, but the director had not called me, hoping to cure him by his own efforts. He did not want me to blame the animal's illness on the zoo.

I ran for a long time through the dark streets, stumbling over cracks in the pavement, slipping in puddles, scaring off lizards and blinks. At the gate I was met by a park attendant. He was sleepy, and his middle eye was closed. I didn't understand what he was saying and ran uphill, past worm cages and enclosures where dim shadows stirred about, wakened by my footsteps.

The tacan lay on the floor in the director's office. The director, in a white coat, sat at the table littered with bottles, ampules, and pillboxes. He was very upset, but I did not stop to console him. The tacan's eyes were covered with a whitish film, like a bird's. His breath came slowly, in gasps, and shivers ran over his skin. When he shivered, his white hooves clattered on the floor.

My first thought was that the dying tacan was dreaming of his blue-gray mountains, but I would not have time enough to take him back. His fur was as soft and warm as ever under my hand, but I knew that it would grow cold before morning. I could not shoot him to end his suffering, because he was my friend.

Suddenly, as if he wanted to say good-by to me, the tacan opened his eyes. But he was looking past me, toward the door. The elder's daughter stood in the doorway.

"I've come," she said. "I guessed from your letter that the tacan was sick. I brought him mountain grass. When longlegs are sick, they eat this grass."

The girl took down the sack she had over her shoulder, and the room filled with the delicate fragrance of mountain meadows and winds.

The tacan said something to her, and the girl drew from the sack an armful of flowers, gray-blue, like the mountains. . . .

Five days later the elder's daughter came to see us off at the cosmodrome. During the days we spent nursing the sick tacan we had become good friends; she trusted me now and believed my promise to take care of him on Earth.

The tacan was still weak, but when the stewardess of the *Orion* saw the three of us coming toward the ship, she squealed with joy, and I said to the tacan:

"You see? I told you."

"I must wake the passengers," cried the stewardess. "They'll think it's a dream. Can he fly?"

"He will," I said. "But don't wake the passengers. They'll have enough time to admire him."

The tacan and I watched the loading of our menagerie. Then we went up to our cabin, where the captain welcomed us. He said it was a breach of rules to have an animal in the passenger section, but he had absolutely nothing against it.

It took us three weeks to reach Earth. During the flight, the tacan made friends with all the passengers and seemed enormously proud of being the center of attention. His wings were now big enough to let him fly along the ship's corridor, and he even took a ten-year-old girl riding on his back.

The girl had with her a book of ancient Greek myths, and I read the tale of Pegasus to the tacan. He repeated some sentences after me and stared at the illustrations, wondering at his resemblance to the hero of the tale.

We agreed that the first appearance of the tacan on Earth must be as dramatic as possible. We dressed the girl in a white cloak like a Greek chlamys and golden sandals. This wasn't easy, for we had to find the materials, then make the costume. The girl's mother and the stewardess spent two days sewing and embroidering the cloak, and I had to make the sandals myself. I spoiled several yards of golden plastic before I got the sandals to fit.

The night before landing, the tacan could not sleep and nervously tapped his hooves on the floor.

"Don't worry," I said to him. "Sleep. Tomorrow will be a difficult day."

When the *Orion* landed and the television cameras were

rolled up to the ship, the tacan went up to the hatch and said to the girl:

"Hold on tight."

"I know," said the girl.

The captain ordered the hatch opened. Cameras whirred, and the crowd in the huge cosmodrome stared at the dark doorway.

I never imagined that the news of our arrival would cause such excitement on Earth. Thousands of people came to the cosmodrome, and the telesatellites that met us at the outer orbit and formed an honor guard, escorting us to the field, circled around us like fat beetles.

The tacan leaped out lightly, rose over the field, and floated slowly toward the open eyes of the television cameras. His wings, thin and transparent, were almost invisible. It merely seemed that the rider was enveloped in a faint mist. The girl raised her arm in greeting.

The tacan seemed to dance before the cameras. He came down close to them, paused for a moment, then soared again and again toward the clouds. The girl held on fast to his mane and gripped his sides with her golden sandals.

"He will not get too tired?" asked the stewardess.

"I don't think he will," I answered, smiling. "He has turned out to be quite vain."

SEVER GANSOVSKY

We Are Not Alone

The noise of the pursuers grew louder, and Naar, gasping for air, thought again: he must ask the Youth to leave him, to run ahead alone. He was too old to keep up. (He did not even know the young man's name—he simply called him Youth.) But suddenly the powerful, low roar which had confounded the whole city at the moment when they left the prison shook the sky and the cliffs again. Then it fell silent.

This time the sound was even stronger—savage, all-engulfing. And it clearly came from above, from the sky.

The Youth, tall and handsome, with stern, attentive eyes, halted and turned to Naar.

"Have you ever heard anything like it, Teacher?"

Naar shook his head. The sound had a slight resemblance to the roaring of a hurricane, but the weather was still and windless. It resembled the rolling of distant thunder, but this time it was short—a quick, violent thud, as though something had approached them from above, from unimaginable distances, struck like a hammer, and vanished back into the sky.

"Never."

The Youth glanced at the sky, then down, into the valley.

The pursuers had also stopped, frightened by the roar.

The decorated ones, with long whips in their hands, and the slaves were scattered in three large groups across the rocky slope. Each group had two fast diatons, but here, on the steep ground, those agile beasts became clumsy. Their middle feet got in the way.

Now everyone stood motionless.

The decorated ones, tall and broad-shouldered (each almost one and a half times taller than a townsman and twice as tall as a slave), stood with their whips lowered and their heads, surmounted by heavy crests, turned up to the gray, tattered sky. The slaves immediately dropped their long, gnarled arms to the ground and rested on all fours. The diatons lay down on the rocks, folding their six legs under them, and turning their long, narrow muzzles from side to side.

Then one of the decorated ones removed his helmet with the crest and waved it above his head. It seemed to Naar he recognized him from the distance. He was the Elder of the House of Judgment and Punishment.

At the Elder's sign, the other decorated ones from all the groups gathered in the center of the valley and formed a circle. From above, the two fugitives could see their lips move: they were discussing something, looking up from time to time. Then they dispersed to their places.

"Forward, Teacher," said the Youth.

They ran again, making their way through the chaos of rocks.

Why did he bring me out of the prison? thought Naar. Can anyone still need me after all these years of torture and pain?

He suddenly realized that he had seen the Youth before. Many days ago he had been taken, as the custom was, to the city square, and one of the decorated ones, driving him on with a whip, kept shouting, "This is the madman who insists that above our sky there is another, bright one! This is he who denies the Universal Stone!" He shouted in that special, nasal tone the decorated ones were trained to use from childhood, to distinguish them further from the townsmen and the slaves. It was then that Naar had noticed the proud, attentive look and the stern young face, and he thought bitterly: Does he despise me, too? But days passed, and this morning the door of his cell was suddenly flung open. The dead guard lay on the floor, and the Youth led him out of the city. What for?

Behind them, they heard whistles and the sharp cracking of whips. The pursuit had been resumed. The fugitives silently increased their pace.

"He calls me Teacher," Naar said to himself. "So there are some who believe me?"

He had almost ceased to believe himself, and what had happened decades ago seemed almost like a dream. He was at that time young and strong, and so tall that in the dark he was mistaken for a decorated one. He therefore could wander about the city at night without fear of being taken to the House of Punishment. Gradually, Naar began to doubt the teachings of the decorated ones. Their science asserted that above their gray, tossing, tattered sky there was an eternal Universal Stone that filled the entire Space of Spaces. That the ocean surrounding the twenty cities was bounded in the distance by the same Universal Stone. That the only life in the world was the life of the twenty cities—the life of the decorated ones, the townsmen, and the slaves. The stone below, and the stone above, over the sky, was all there was and all there would ever be.

But once, wandering along the shore, Naar saw the heavy waves cast onto the rocks a marvelous, hard grass that did not grow anywhere within the area of the twenty cities. Later, in the caves of the fishermen who supplied the decorated ones with fish that they caught by hand, Naar often saw mats and baskets made of the same grass, and discovered that the fisherman believed that there were other lands beyond the ocean, and, possibly, other cities as well. It was then that he began to doubt the teaching about the Universal Stone. He asked himself why the sky was brighter in the daytime, and dark at night, why its color was forever changing, how living beings had come to exist in the hollow space between the stones. And then, tormented by these questions, he decided to climb to the sky, to ascend the Mountain of all Mountains, whose summit, according to the science of the decorated ones, was joined to the Universal Stone.

It was a marvelous journey. He went higher and higher, surmounting the steeps and rising over deep abysses. At first his only food was the coarse moss that grew on rocks and was the sole food of the slaves. Then, faint with hunger, he came upon a nest of honey-making birds. Naar knew that honey was the food of the decorated ones and was deadly to townsmen and slaves. But he was so exhausted that he ventured to break one egg in the nest and to drink it. Instead of harming him, the honey gave him strength, although he was not one of the decorated.

From the height he saw five cities all at once, and they looked like small heaps of pebbles.

Later, on the third eight-day period of his journey, Naar

reached the sky. And it turned out to be just like the fog that gathered in the evenings among the cliffs by the ocean. Naar went higher and higher. The swirls of fog turned into a billowing gray mass, and the valley below was no longer visible. Naar had already begun to think that soon he would reach the Universal Stone. But the fog around him and over him began to thin. It became lighter. The terrible cold that had tormented him as he climbed gave way to warmth. And, finally, during the fifth eight-day period, a great miracle happened. The gray sky of clouds and fog lay as an endless plain beneath him. And high above him, everywhere, there was another sky, splendid, deep, blue and radiant. In this sky burned a huge disk, so bright it almost blinded Naar as he looked up at it. The disk's rays warmed him, lent him new strength.

And there was no Universal Stone. The disk rose over Naar's head, the blue sky stretched into illimitable heights, the mountaintops around were covered with grasses, dense and vivid, such as he had never seen below, and birds sang. And the world that remained under the layer of fog and clouds, the world of decorated ones and their slaves, suddenly seemed to Naar dark, terrible, and pitiful.

But later, when Naar came down and began to talk to people in the cities about what he had seen, the decorated ones seized him, and under torture in the chambers of the House of Punishment he had almost begun to disbelieve what his own eyes had seen.

"Teacher," said the Youth. "Lean on me." He had noticed that Naar walked with difficulty, and took him by the hand. "Teacher, I brought you out of prison to show you something. Many of the young believe you, and several of us decided to repeat your great journey. We held secret gatherings here, on the rocky plateau, to keep the decorated ones from learning our intention. And many days ago, when we, the shepherds, were here, we heard the sound—the same sound that we heard today. A shining sphere flew out of the sky and fell nearby. The noise was shattering, and stones flew up, then everything was quiet. When we approached the spot, we found a heavy object with a strange mark on it. We picked it up and saw that it was polished, as only the hands of reason could polish an object. We want to show it to you, and you will tell us what you think it means. Friends are waiting for us in our gathering place; we shall escape the pursuit and hide in the mountains. . . ."

He had barely finished when a whistling sound came from the left and an arrow flew over their heads. Glancing back, they saw a new group of pursuers: in the center, three decorated ones, the crests on their helmets flowing in the wind; on either side of them, a long chain of slaves, bending in rapid movement. Some ran on two feet, others helped themselves with their hands. One of them was already so near that Naar could see the cunning smile on his face. The slave was hoping to be the first to seize him; for this he would be rewarded by much food.

There was also whistling on the right, and a new group appeared on the plateau.

"Run, Teacher!" cried the Youth. He pushed Naar toward a narrow path between huge boulders. "Run. Our people will meet you there." And he lay down among the rocks, preparing his bow and arrows.

Naar took several steps, and halted. What for? He would not escape. His body was weak. During the torture at the House of Punishment many muscles had been torn from his arms and legs.

"Look, look!" one of the decorated ones cried out in his nasal voice. "There he is, there is the madman who says that there is something else above our sky!"

Hastily, the Youth pulled at his bow and released an arrow. But the arrow merely tore the crest from the helmet of the decorated one. Frightened and astounded, the pursuer stopped and looked around.

The other decorated ones also stopped.

"Horror! Horror!" they cried. "He raised his hand against the all-powerful."

The slave who was already a few paces from the Youth leaped forward, stretching out his arms. He was struck by the Youth's second arrow. Pierced through, he fell upon the rocks, biting the arrow and trying to tear it out of his body.

Naar ran back and lay down next to the Youth.

"*You* must run," he said. "Run, or they'll take you to the House of Punishment."

The Youth turned sharply to him.

"Why are you still here? Hurry!"

The decorated ones cracked their whips again. Now they drove the slaves before them, while they themselves took shelter behind rocks.

"Fear and tremble! Fear and tremble!" came a nasal cry, and Naar recognized the Elder.

At that moment the Youth seized Naar by the shoulder.

"Listen, Teacher! Again!"

The air shook around them, and a distant roar came from above, where, Naar knew, an endless blue sky stretched high above the clouds. The sound grew; now it was twice as loud as the first two times—it was becoming unendurable.

The slaves and the decorated ones halted. Everyone looked up in terror.

Something dark appeared over them in the clouds. It became larger and larger, and suddenly a huge, long object came out of the murk. Spewing flame from behind, it was descending from the sky, still growing larger. For a moment it stood still over the heaps of rock, then it came down and settled three hundred paces from Naar and his companion.

The decorated ones and the slaves threw themselves down upon the ground.

"Look!" cried the Youth, standing up. "The same mark on it that we saw the other day! The same!"

This happened long ago, in the year when the first ship from Earth broke through the eternal cloud cover that sheathes Venus.

VLADLEN BAKHNOV

Twelve Holidays

[ONE]

Only the stern sense of duty and the extraordinary patience that characterize all true time pilots made me agree to undertake this strange assignment.

One day the World Science Council sent me on a mission on timecraft MV 20–64 into the past of a certain small country. I have no right to reveal its name or location. We shall therefore call it Yonia. I was sent there at the highly confidential request of the prime minister of Yonia, who desperately needed assistance.

However, as soon as I arrived, I realized that no one could really help that wretched country because it was ruled by a king, whose name must also remain secret. Let us call him Alfonse.

And to give a true idea of what Alfonse was like, I can say without the slightest exaggeration that if he had been placed at the head of the wealthiest great power he would undoubtedly have turned it within three years into one of the most underdeveloped countries in the world.

Yonia's worst problem was not that the king spent more money than he had, or permitted himself things that should never be permitted to anyone, or forbade others things that should never be forbidden. . . . If those were his only faults, Alfonse would not have been too different from any of his predecessors.

No, the most dangerous thing for the country was the king's habit of suddenly conceiving brilliant ideas on how to raise his kingdom to everlasting greatness. Alfonse stubbornly tried to heap all kinds of blessings on Yonia, and labored without sparing himself, not to speak of his subjects, for the good of his country.

If the young king had an inspiration on Monday, the inspiration was law on Tuesday. On Wednesday, the law was enforced, and on Thursday the heads of violators were flying right and left.

After a month or two, the new law would somehow lapse into oblivion. But heads continued to fly, because by then a still newer law would have been proclaimed. And, as they said in Yonia, "all you need is a law, and there will never be a lack of violators."

Naturally, the king never consulted anyone when he devised his innovations. True, he was surrounded by counselors and sages, but in Yonia counselors earned their title only by listening to the king's counsel; and sages, by nodding sagely every time the king spoke.

No wonder the creative ideas of the young monarch had such destructive power.

One might ask what an expert time pilot could do in backward Yonia. And why its prime minister had asked for me. But it was a good thing I came. And the prime minister knew what he was doing.

Let me explain my duties. Every time the king issued a new law, which was always to make his subjects the happiest men on earth, I would get into my time ship and travel to the nearest future. There I would find out what misfortunes would be heaped upon the kingdom as a result of the law, and return to make my report to the prime minister. That misfortunes would come was never doubted by anyone except Alfonse. But it was important to discover their exact nature, so that the minister could then at least try to prepare for them.

This was my extraordinary assignment in that unhappy kingdom. And it had to be performed in utmost secrecy. The king had no suspicion of my activities or even my existence. But I realized that sooner or later Alfonse was bound to find out, and then. . . .

Well, in the end it happened.

[TWO]

One day the prime minister summoned me and said:

"Get ready for a trip. His Majesty has thought up a new law. This time he expects it to result in universal and ever-expanding prosperity in the country." And the minister showed me a document entitled "The Law of the Twelve Holidays."

"From this day on," the document stated, "a new system shall come into effect in Yonia, designed to bring about total prosperity in the shortest possible time. It shall be known as 'The System of Obligatory Gifts' under 'The Law of the Twelve Holidays.'

"The holidays shall be celebrated monthly.

"Each citizen MUST give presents every month to no fewer than twenty fellow citizens, and MUST receive from them gifts of equal value.

"In order to assure steady production of various gifts,

factories and plants will be set up throughout the kingdom, eliminating unemployment and raising the well-being of the country to ever-higher levels.

"As the living standard rises, the citizens of Yonia will be able to offer one another more and more expensive gifts, and this, in turn, will result in still greater prosperity.

"Since the demand for gift items will grow from month to month, more and more factories will be built and soon the kingdom will become a mighty industrial power rivaling only the United States of America.

"Within two or three years, The Law of the Twelve Holidays will bring Yonia into an era of total prosperity and universal well-being.

"To be proclaimed at once,

King Alfonse the First."

I returned the document to the prime minister. He carefully put it away in a fireproof safe, and asked me to take a short trip into the future as soon as possible.

"I can't imagine what all of this will lead to," he said.

I promised to set out on my mission at dawn the next morning and make a detailed study of the coming disasters.

The disasters, however, began that very same night. And the events that followed were too incredible to be foreseen, even by me.

[THREE]

I was certain that no one except the prime minister knew about my work. But everything turned out to be much more complicated.

The point is that Yonia had been on bad terms for over a century with neighboring Xonia (the name is, of course, fictional). They had even waged war several times, but without result, since their forces were equal, or, to put it more precisely, since both countries were equally weak.

With the coming of Alfonse all this had changed. After the king's very first innovations, the rulers of Xonia realized an important political fact: if no one interfered with Alfonse, he would himself reduce Yonia to such a state that it could then be taken with bare hands.

The prime minister of Xonia prayed fervently that Alfonse remain on the throne as long as possible. But he knew that prayer alone was not enough: Alfonse might be overthrown at any moment either by his heirs, in their haste to seize power, or by his desperate ministers, or even by his subjects, brought to the end of their endurance.

To prevent this, the prime minister of Xonia established a super-secret Committee for the Protection of Enemy No. 1. The Committee dispatched to Yonia a thousand of the most experienced agents, whose task it was to protect Alfonse without his knowledge from all internal enemies: mutineers, rebels, plotters, relatives, court physicians, even the royal guard. Not a single person in Yonia knew about these agents. And, at the risk of their own lives, they guarded their worst enemy day and night.

Even secrets unsuspected by Yonia's police and intelligence service became known to the agents of the Committee for the Protection of the Enemy.

When the prime minister of Xonia became curious as to why Alfonse's latest laws were not harming Yonia as they should, the agents of the Committee launched an investigation and found out about my trips into the future.

Under orders from the premier of Xonia, they sent an anonymous letter to King Alfonse, exposing the secret actions of his own prime minister. In this way, they hoped to get rid of both me and the king's highest official at one fell stroke.

Well, although their cunning plans were only partly successful, their letter had nevertheless saved long-suffering Yonia from further misfortune.

[FOUR]

Now, this is what happened.

On the night after I learned about the Law of the Twelve Holidays, I received a visit from two men who declared that the king wished to see me at once.

"I am sorry that my officers have wakened you," Alfonse said politely as soon as I was led in.

"It doesn't matter, Your Majesty," I answered just as politely. "I'll have time to catch up on my sleep."

"I'm not so sure of that," the king said playfully, and gave me an attentive look. "Doesn't it seem to you, Mr. Lozhkin, that my ministers, who were sending you into the future, were not entirely convinced of the wisdom of my ideas?"

"I think, Your Majesty, that you'd do better to put this question to the ministers themselves."

"Alas, that is no longer possible," Alfonse said with a melancholy sigh. "You see, if I did not believe that my ideas would make Yonia a happier place, I simply could not live any longer. And my ministers did not believe in the future, and therefore they could not live any longer."

"What do you mean?" I asked.

"Just that," the king answered. "After all, you are an alien, and you will never understand our patriotism. I hope you're not offended?"

The king was a well-bred man.

"I have a small request to make of you," Alfonse went on. "I trust it will not seem too burdensome."

"I'm listening."

"I am extremely concerned about the future of my Yonia, and I'm most anxious to see it flourishing and happy—as it is sure to be in the nearest future. But we are all mortal. And I would be very grieved if I were to die without seeing the fruit of my labors. I would therefore like to take a trip in your timecraft, to about fifty years or so from now. I'm sure it will be possible, won't it?"

"No, Your Majesty. The rules of the World Science Council expressly forbid time pilots to ferry any outsiders."

"Rules, rules! Let's not be pedants, Mr. Lozhkin."

"No, Your Majesty, they'll take away my pilot's license."

"They won't. No one will know about our trip except the two of us. It will be our little secret."

"I can't!"

"Forgive me, Mr. Lozhkin, but I must repeat that, unfortunately, all of us are mortal. And it would seem to me that keeping your head ought to be more important to you than keeping your pilot's license. . . . Hmm, I am so witty today!"

So that's it! I thought. He wants to scare me! Oh, well, to the devil with him! Let this tyrant glance into the future, let him hear what grateful posterity will say about him! It may even do him some good.

"Very well," I said. "Your Majesty has convinced me. But I beg that nobody be told about our journey."

"The word of a king," said Alfonse solemnly. We stole out of the palace and departed into the future.

At that time I did not know about the Committee for the Protection of the Enemy, and I am puzzled to this day how we managed to escape the attention of its omnipresent agents. A happy chance—if the king still thinks of it as happy.

I must say that, during my stay in Yonia, I never went more than five years ahead. There was simply no need to. But this time we skipped half a century at once. Alfonse, who was not used to time travel, got dizzy. And I—I gasped with astonishment as I stepped out of the timecraft.

I would never have thought that Yonia—impoverished, wretched Yonia—could change so much.

The people in the streets were gay and smiling. From the way they spoke to each other, without glancing over their shoulders and without hiding their eyes, it was clear that they had nobody to be afraid of.

The wide, green street stretched far into the distance. On either side of it rose bright and airy buildings, where only happy people could live.

"You see!" Alfonse said proudly. "You see how fine and prosperous my country has become. It shows I succeeded in forcing my subjects to be happy. And all thanks to the Twelve Holidays, I assure you. I had a feeling that it was the most brilliant idea I'd ever had, and I was right! I can imagine how posterity respects and honors my memory, if I'm already, God forbid, dead. And incidentally, Mr. Lozhkin, how can we find out whether I'm still here?"

"We can ask any passerby."

"Oh, no! If I am alive, then such a question will land us right in prison. Imagine, asking whether a living king is still alive!"

Then I proposed putting the question in a different form, and stopped an old man who was walking by:

"Would you please tell us where we can find King Alfonse?"

"I certainly won't!" the old man replied with an astonished glance, and hurried on.

"What could that mean?" the king wondered. "Could I have ordered that my whereabouts be kept secret?"

"That's for you to know," I said, and stopped a passing schoolboy. "Where does King Alfonse live?"

"I know of no such king."

"What do you mean you know of no such king?" Alfonse asked sternly.

"Oh—we haven't studied about him yet," the boy explained and ran on, swinging his school bag.

"What a rude boy!" Alfonse said with displeasure. "A pity I didn't execute his father, or, still better, his grandfather!"

The next passerby was a college student.

"Of course I know about King Alfonse," he said, and my companion proudly raised his head. "Alfonse was our last king."

"Last?" The king frowned.

"He brought the country to such a state of ruin that the citizens of Yonia decided to manage without kings in the future."

"And?"

"And they did."

"And what did they do with Alfonse?" Alfonse asked.

"They didn't have to do anything with him. He simply disappeared one fine day."

"Disappeared? Disappeared where?"

"Nobody knows. All we know is that he executed all his ministers, and then he disappeared himself. They looked for him, but he was never found. But then, they didn't look too hard, and nobody cried over his disappearance. Everybody was sick and tired of him."

"Ah, so that's how it was!" said Alfonse as soon as the student left. "I see! They were sick and tired of me? Well, now I know everything, and I'll be sure to take preventive measures. Imagine, my personal guard! I disappear, and they don't even know where. Just wait, they'll disappear before they know it! But still, it would be interesting to find out where I could have disappeared to, don't you think?"

But only one man in the world knew the answer to his question—myself.

I saw what I must do while the student was still talking about the strange disappearance of Yonia's last king. And when Alfonse spoke of preventive measures, my last doubts vanished.

A moment, and I was back in my timecraft. I slammed the door in the king's face, and switched on the reverse, at top speed.

Two days later all Yonia was agog. Everybody talked about the king's mysterious disappearance. But since no one knew about our trip, they looked for Alfonse everywhere except in the future.

And Alfonse meantime ran through the streets of the capital, shouting that he was Alfonse.

I know from the most reliable sources that he finally landed in a hosptial where, in addition to him, there were several other Alfonses, Napoleons, and Nebuchadnezzars.

At first, my conscience troubled me. Then I recalled that I had been sent to Yonia to help that poor country. And after all, what help could have been better than ridding it of its last king?

MIKHAIL YEMTSEV & YEREMEY PARNOV

The White Pilot

You may have heard about the Galápagos pilot. People called him the White Pilot. There were many articles in newspapers and magazines at the time, both about Kidd and Lindall, and much nonsense was written about them. I can tell you what really happened. I studied at Oxford with Percival Lindall, and we planned to take this trip to the Galápagos—the Tortoise Islands—together. Even the idea of the ultrahydrophone, which Lindall constructed later, was originally mine. But nothing came of our plan. At least, not at the time. Lindall married a girl we were both in love with, and I left for Melbourne, to work in the National Oceanological Laboratory.

Nevertheless, Lindall did not abandon his old dream. He left his wife with his parents in Glasgow, crossed the ocean, and went to Ecuador. Thanks to some letters of recommendation and his personal charm, he was able to outfit an expedition. But, then, expedition is perhaps too big a word for it. All he had was a tiny cutter with a cramped little cabin, several cases of canned food and beer, two rifles, some swimming and diving gear, and, of course, the hydrophone, a stock of dry-cell batteries, and a few personal trifles. The cutter's name was *Galápagos*. In this flimsy vessel, under the splendid red, blue, and yellow Ecuadorean flag, Lindall set out into the Pacific Ocean.

A local teacher was to have gone with him, but at the last minute he pleaded illness, and Lindall went alone. During the day he steered the little ship, and at night, when the weather was calm, he cast anchor and settled down to sleep right on the deck, under cover of a sheet and the Southern Cross.

On one such night Lindall was wakened by a bright light. The white ray of a searchlight nailed the *Galápagos* to the surface of the ocean like an insect to the board of a collection. When Lindall stood up, the ray quivered and slid off to the side. Some fifty yards from his ship he saw the black silhouette of a submarine, bristling at him with a cannon and two machine guns.

"Who are you?" a man on the bridge asked through a loudspeaker in slightly accented English.

"A research ship. . . . Registered for Guayaquil. . . . And who are you?"

"Crew?" the man asked, ignoring his question.

"By what right are you interrogating me in extraterritorial waters?"

"Answer, or we'll sink you."

Lindall shrugged, found the cigarettes in his pocket, and lit one.

"How many men on your ship?"

"I'm alone."

"Alone?" The man bent over the hatch and spoke to someone. Then he shouted through the loudspeaker.

"We'll pay you a visit! But don't try to resist, or you'll be sunk immediately."

A small rowboat emerged from under the submarine's

shadow and slid lightly and silently toward the *Galápagos*. The speaker and another man were in it. When they boarded, Lindall gestured them toward the cabin, but the cabin was too small, and they made themselves at home on deck. Lindall immediately recognized them as Germans.

"The ship's documents!"

After examining them, the Germans moved away and began to discuss something. The officer who had first spoken tried heatedly to convince his companion, a tall, blond man, of something, but the latter shook his head.

They came back to Lindall and the tall man asked:

"Are you English?"

"American," said Lindall. It was 1939, and he knew that war was imminent. "My grandfather left Germany and settled in Boston."

"He was German?"

"Yes."

The Germans exchanged glances.

"Do you have a lifeboat?" asked the tall man.

Lindall nodded.

"Fine. We'll give you forty minutes. Load everything essential into the lifeboat and sail toward the coast."

"The coast?" Lindall repeated. "But we're more than six hundred miles from the continent. . . ."

"Why the continent?" the officer laughed. "The ship's log says you are bound for the Galápagos Islands. Well, that's where you can go. They're only about a hundred miles away."

"But . . . that's simply murder!" Lindall still failed to understand what they were after.

"No more talk! Get ready and consider yourself lucky. We can use your tub."

Lindall loaded his provisions into the lifeboat.

"May I take the rifle?"

"What for?" The officer put his hand on the gun.

"Let him have it," the tall one said. "And what's this?" He pointed to the ultrahydrophone that Lindall brought from the cabin.

"An apparatus for catching the sounds made by marine animals."

"Something to worry about!" The officer laughed again. "Afraid you won't find a common language with the fish?"

"Let him alone, Manfred," said the tall man. "Leave the log and the documents here. Ready?"

Lindall nodded and stepped into the lifeboat, which was suspended on the dark side of the *Galápagos.* The tackle creaked and soon he was rocking on the waves. It seemed to him he was at the bottom of a black well. He looked up. The Ecuadorean flag was a narrow silver strip in the inky sky. The huge tropical stars seemed closer than ever. Lindall pushed off and took the oars. His fingers trembled.

"Happy sailing, friend!" cried the officer.

Lindall silently rowed away from the *Galápagos,* straight toward the Southern Cross.

Before long, he was caught up by an arm of the Peruvian Stream and carried northward. According to his calculations, he was to see the volcanic cones of the Tortoise Islands on the ninth day. He hoped to land either on Española or on Santa Maria. But toward morning of the ninth day a dense fog fell over the sea. It seemed to Lindall that he could hear the surf against the rocks, but he could see nothing. He steered west. The noise on his left did not subside, and on the right it didn't get louder. He turned the boat eastward. The fog was so thick that even the stern of the boat looked blurred and ghostly. Lindall was no longer sure of his bearings. He no longer worried that the boat might be smashed against invisible rocks; he was afraid of missing land. And when the noise of the surf began to recede, he realized that the worst had happened—he was being carried out into the open ocean. It was impossible to row his way back against the strong current. He recalled that there was still a tiny island somewhere nearby, but the chance of hitting upon it in the fog was minimal. Nevertheless, Lindall decided to try. He turned the boat around and began to row against the current. Now his northward progress was considerably slowed, and he could still hope to find some signs by which he might determine his position with regard to the island. Hours went by. Lindall was dead tired and ready to abandon the oars and lie down in the boat, submitting himself to providence. But suddenly he thought he heard the characteristic, guttural cries of cormorants. These large birds have underdevoloped wings; it was clear, then, that land must be near. Lindall listened. It seemed that the cries grew louder. He dropped the oars and took up the steering wheel. Behind the thick gray curtain the sun was visible only as a brighter spot. But slowly, gradually, the fog began to melt away.

Standing up in his boat, Lindall caught sight of the dark edge and sharp summits of a volcanic range. They seemed to hang suspended in the air, cut off by the horizontal line of fog. The line descended slowly; the fog was disappearing like water down a sluiceway. Lindall bit his lips. To his impatient eyes, the gray veil seemed almost motionless. The bird cries became deafening. The boat moved rapidly toward the shore.

Lindall knew that the approaches to the small uninhabited islands were extremely dangerous. The islands were surrounded by broken chains of underground reefs. But he had no choice. Besides, he hoped that the light boat would slip in safely above the reefs. This time he was in luck. Before he realized it, he was past the danger zone. The water around him grew warmer. The fog lay on its surface like a milky sheet. The lowering gray-blue cliffs looked alien and unwelcoming. Their sheer slopes were mercilessly crisscrossed with deep gashes and covered with black, crumpled streams of petrified lava.

Lindall wondered whether Darwin would ever have written his *Origin of Species* if the *Beagle* had not cast anchor within sight of these gloomy, inhospitable volcanoes. The thought made him feel a little better. He knew that the islands were not quite as bare and unwelcoming as they looked.

The noise of the birds drowned out even the thunder of the surf. Of the eighty-nine species of birds nesting here, seventy-seven were not to be found anywhere else on earth. They seemed to Lindall to have gathered there to greet him, and despite all he felt happy. He had dreamed of the Galápagos for so many years. Not every man lives to see his dream come true.

Lindall took up the oars and rowed eagerly toward shore, looking for a landing spot. Now he clearly saw a school of marine iguanas. The prehistoric dragons with sharp ridged backs were warming themselves upon the rocks, sprayed by the rapid inflowing tide. The foam blistered the rock and dried like a thin soapy crust. Thousands of birds searched for food in the decaying black seaweed, leaped over the basalt shingle, brooded on their eggs. A pair of sea lions gamboled in the cool water of the current that circled the island. Black, shiny, as though wearing tight rubber suits, they raised their whiskered muzzles to the sky, leaped up, and disappeared amid the waves. Then they appeared again, threw silver, glistening fish into the air, caught them in mid-flight, and dived down for more.

Lindall rowed along the line of the tide. He was impatient to go ashore, make a fire, and drink some hot coffee, but it was difficult to find a suitable landing place.

When he was almost at the end of his patience and strength—he was just rounding a volcanic promontory—he caught sight of a level strip of shingle. The waves rolled up the shore and, slithering over the stones, ran far inland, only to stream back at once in thousands of hissing rivulets.

Lindall tightened his grip on the oars. His blistered palms burned mercilessly. Those last moments, as he rowed toward shore, seemed longer than all the hours he had spent face to face with the sea. Finally, the pebbles clattered under the boat, and it stopped. With an effort, Lindall straightened his fingers. Then he lay down on the floor of the boat and looked into the sky.

Under the very clouds, his great, powerful wings spread wide, soared a frigate bird. Lindall closed his swollen, tearing eyes and fell asleep. At the very last moment the thought flashed through his mind that he must not sleep long, or the ebb tide would carry him back to the sea or wreck the boat on the reefs. He even made an effort to get up and out of the boat, but sleep overcame him, plunging him into a heavy nightmare that was frighteningly close to reality. Lindall dreamed that he had stepped out of the boat and, groaning with pain, was dragging it over the clattering shingle farther away from the sea. But just as he had brought it to the foot of the volcano and, straightening his numb back, glanced over his shoulder, the German officer suddenly appeared, with a cane in his hands. Swinging the cane, he pointed with his gloved hand at the sea. And Lindall understood that he must drag the boat back and again row somewhere to an unknown destination. With bleeding fingers he grasped the wet, salty boards and pulled at them, while the officer laughed. And the greater Lindall's pain, the more the officer laughed. Then Lindall abandoned the boat, fell flat upon the shingle, gathered the last of his strength, and woke up.

Dazedly he stared at the shore, at the foot of the volcano. The sun was lower now. The ebbing water roared and whistled, rolling back over the stones.

Lindall climbed out of the boat and dragged it with difficulty to higher ground. His body ached. A heavy stupor pressed down on his skull. Slowly he walked along the moist, thundering shingle. At every step he made, quick bright little crabs scuttled to their holes. But the birds were unafraid. They ran about busily right at his feet. A hawk that had been soaring overhead plummeted down, apparently out of sheer curiosity, and alighting nearby, began to study him with round eyes.

Lindall found a narrow cleft between two streams of hardened lava. Grasping at the rough surface, he began to climb. Every now and then he stopped and lay down to rest.

The first opuntias appeared. As he went up, there were more and more of them. Lindall looked with wonder at the large, bluish trees with their fleshy, thorny trunks. When he reached the top and saw a wooded plateau, Lindall sighed with relief. The dense, green crowns of graceful scalesias, the red trunks of pisonias, the luxuriant ferns—all of this promised rest and peace.

Above the trees loomed the summit of the volcano, veiled in mist. Lindall knew that the crater held a deep, cold lake with vivid blue-green water. He felt like a man who had returned after a long absence to his beloved, half-forgotten homeland. He saw everything here for the first time, but he had read and dreamed so much about it that he recognized the trees and the rocks, and he greeted them like old friends. And they replied to him. The long strands of dark-green moss suspended from the branches waved to him. The birds trustingly allowed themselves to be picked up. The rocks were warm, and the sea calm.

Lindall smiled, raising his face to the sky. He shouted, and the shout came hoarsely from his strained, sore throat. Then he climbed down rapidly, raked together a pile of sun-dried seaweed on the shore, and made a fire. He boiled some coffee, heated a can of beef, soaked a few biscuits in hot water, and ate his first meal of the day. Everything was marvelously tasty. A penguin waddled up and watched him, with head bent to the side. Lindall threw him a piece of biscuit. Unhurriedly, with great dignity, the penguin picked it up, nodded as if to say "thanks," and withdrew. Lindall put out the fire with a few cans of water, smoked a cigarette, and, with his head in the shadow of a huge basalt boulder, went to sleep.

His first year on the island was spent in solitary work. He hunted wild pigs, fished, looked for tortoise eggs, cooked crabs. For hours he wandered on the shore in search of interesting marine animals. From time to time he would examine the mollusks clinging to slippery stones or pull tiny octopi from fissures in the rocks. He built himself a small, comfortable cabin at the edge of the woods. Inside, it was always fresh and cool. The red pisonia wood filled the air with a delicate fragrance. At the entrance, large ferns swayed their fronds.

Every day Lindall went out to sea for three or four hours. He lowered the ultrahydrophone over shallow spots, put on his earphones, and immersed himself in the world of sounds. He heard the constant clicking of innumerable alpheus lobsters, the rhythmic purring of sea robins, the dovelike moans of slabs, the barking and grunting of yellowfin croakers. Sometimes the individual sounds were drowned out by the usual medley of noises. Lindall knew what was behind them; mentally he saw the teeth of fish and crabs' claws crushing and crumbling branches of coral and mollusk shells—the constant chewing and swallowing, the unending pursuit. The range of sounds normally heard by man is pitifully small. Every time Lindall switched on the ultrahydrophone, he was astonished anew by the diversity of whistling, buzzing, howling, and humming tones.

Sometimes he dived down himself. Earphones protected by his watertight helmet, he cautiously stole up to the fish. There was probably no one in the world who knew more about communication among fish, their warning signals, their ways of letting each other know where food was to be found.

Lindall worked long hours, leaving himself little free time. But increasingly he began to catch himself longing for people, for simple conversation with another human being. He was unable to leave the island at will, and this intensified his loneliness. If his tiny *Galápagos* were rocking quietly on the waves of some inlet with its tank full of fuel, Lindall would probably have spent at least another year without thought of the civilized world. But his ship was not there, and Lindall often watched the horizon, searching for the smoke of a passing steamer. It never appeared.

One night he heard the droning of planes at a great height. Quickly, he made a fire with dry scalesia branches. The flames ran up the ether-saturated stems. A hospital smell spread in the air. The bright flames dimmed the stars. The noise of the planes died down. And for a long time Lindall lived in the hope that his signal had been noticed. But months went by, and no one came for him. Lindall plunged again into his work. He wrote articles for scientific journals, sorted his rolls of film, dissected marine animals, studied the roots of local plants, and melted down the fat of huge, elephantine tortoises. But more and more often he would put his work aside and stare at the faint bluish line of the horizon.

Not to forget human speech, Lindall talked to himself. He recited poems and dramatic monologues, and even composed one-act plays for two characters. He spoke constantly, until his throat ran dry. Then he drank the cooled juice of sweet ferns, and spoke again. Even as he dived with his ultrahydrophone, he never stopped talking. The fish had grown so used to him that they no longer paid him any attention. And he hovered around them, listening to their secrets and immediately translating them aloud, or reciting poems.

The solitary human body slid noiselessly through the ghostly blue water, above the swaying forests of seaweed, under the dark roofs of caverns. Over him flowed beads of quicksilver, beneath him flashed the shadows of birds that made the sleepy fish dart off in fear. But the man spoke and spoke, and the fish listened to the jeweled lines of Shakespeare, the stately verse of Tennyson, the hypnotic music of Swinburne, and the assonances of Browning. The fish swam out of dark grottoes, out of the luxuriant growths of seaweed. The man listened to fish tales and talked, talked, talked.

One day, after a solid breakfast of tortoise meat and baked fern, Lindall swung the ultrahydrophone over his shoulder, took his fins, and went down, as he usually did, to the sea. A warm morning breeze stirred the air. The glasslike water fleas had come far up the shore. This tokened stormy weather, but Lindall decided to chance it. It had been raining for four days and he thought gloomily of the long hours spent in the cabin. Lindall pushed the boat into the water, slipped the oars into the locks, and rowed leeward. As he was rounding the promontory, which jutted far into the sea, the sun rose. The sea glittered with a thousand dazzling sparks. Lindall felt warm and sleepy. He dipped his palm into the sea and dashed the cold water on his face. The world became transformed, glowing with every color of the rainbow.

Far out in the sea a flock of gulls darted back and forth with piercing cries over some motionless object. Now and then they settled on the water, folding their wings, only to rise again.

That's odd, thought Lindall. What can it be? A dead whale perhaps?

He rowed toward the spot where the gulls were circling. It was not a dead whale. On the surface of the sea floated the green carcass of a giant squid. The animal was dying. Its color turned from green to vivid purple, then delicately cream. From time to time the drooping tentacles rose and whipped the water to a foam, like the propellers of an ocean liner. The huge, uncomfortably human eyes spoke of mortal distress and pain. It seemed to Lindall that the squid looked at him, pleading for help. But what could he do? Some vital organ of the animal must have been injured, and it could not escape to its underwater home. The gulls seemed to be holding a wake for it while it was still alive; they knew it was doomed.

Lindall lowered the ultrahydrophone into the water. Then he put on his goggles, adjusted the ear pieces, and cautiously dived in from the stern of the boat. The greenish water was marvelously transparent. From below, the squid's huge suckers with their sharp claws looked still more terrifying. Its tentacles were as thick as logs.

Here, too, preparations were in progress for the feast. Whole schools of fish darted by at the squid's very tail, which looked like a plumed torpedo. Golden mackerel kept their distance, but were obviously ready to claim their share of the booty. An ugly surgeon fish was already nipping the dying giant, and a vivid sea robin managed to bite out a piece of flesh.

The squid had evidently taken the man for a new enemy. With a last effort, it gathered up its tentacles and dashed away. The water suddenly grew dark and turbid. Lindall dived down to the bottom for his hydrophone and swam after the squid. The animal did not go far. After letting out its ink, it became pallid and ghostlike, and for a moment Lindall could not see it. But the entire gang of fish was already around it. Even the most timid and cautious hurried to catch up with the exhausted quarry.

When a dark-blue torpedo appeared nearby, Lindall thought it was a shark. Sharks seldom miss such grand funerals, and he had been expecting them. But it turned out to be a large and aggressive dolphin. Learning over the ultrasonic telegraph about the death agony of the immemorial enemy of dolphins, he could not resist the temptation and came to do battle. Without waiting for the squid to die, the dolphin rushed to attack. Lindall did not expect the squid to have enough fight left, but the giant suddenly wrapped the dolphin with three tentacles. The captive tried to break away, but the tentacles tightened around him. Lindall swam rapidly to help the foolhardy attacker. The dolphin did not even struggle, immobilized like a rabbit in the coils of an anaconda. Lindall tried to chop off with his knife the most dangerous tentacle, the tip of which was thrashing in the water. After several blows he succeeded. Coiling like the tail of an enormous lizard, it sank to the bottom. Schools of fish dashed after it. From a dark cavern floated out a spotted, scarflike creature. Lindall caught sight of an open, toothed maw and recognized the moray. He shivered with revulsion. Pale-blue blood rose like thin smoke from the severed tentacle.

When Lindall managed to chop off another tentacle and free the dolphin, the animal was almost breathless. His body was covered with the terrible marks of the squid's suckers.

Lindall put his arms around the dolphin and rose with him to the surface. He climbed into his boat, pulled up the hydrophone, and busied himself with the animal. He wanted to tie him to the boat and bring him ashore. On second thought, he decided that, since some of his batteries still worked, he had no need as yet of dolphin fat, and that, in any case, the valiant madman deserved the right to live. From his pouch he took a needle with a strong silk thread and tried to sew up the dolphin's gaping wounds. Then, when the animal showed the first signs of life, he slapped him on the back and pushed him away from the boat.

The dolphin lay in the water, dazed. Lindall gave him a careful shove with his oar. The dolphin stirred and, flipping his tail on the water, began to swim. He made a circle around the boat and settled down to follow behind it.

Lindall saw that the wind was gathering strength and bore down on the oars. A storm was rising and he hurried home. The dolphin kept up with him, but the man no longer paid him any attention. He recited loudly verses from Swinburne's "Atalanta in Calydon":

> "And thunder of storm on the sands,
> And wailing of waves on the shore. . . .
> Fierce air and violent light,
> Sail rent and sundering oar,
> Darkness and noises of night.
> Clashing of streams in the sea,
> Wave against wave as a sword,
> Clamour of currents and foam. . . ."

"Well, where are you going, silly?" Lindall asked the dolphin. The boat had passed the line of underwater reefs, and now it was but a short way to the promontory. But the dolphin still refused to leave his rescuer. It was only when they had almost reached the shore that he leaped up in the air, and then swam out into the open sea to meet the rising waves.

It was not until three days later that the ocean calmed down and the water brightened. Lindall set up the ultrahydrophone at the entrance to a grotto densely overgrown with small mollusks. Sensing the presence of an enemy, the shells clamped shut and did not open until the man, dragging the thin red wire after him, rose to the surface. The water was warm, and Lindall did not feel like returning to the boat. He floated on his back and, lazily stirring his fins, gazed at the pure morning sky. There was a low whistling in his earphones, alternating between high and low frequencies. Lindall closed his eyes and surrendered himself to pleasant languor, certain that he would not hear anything particularly interesting that day. The anchored rowboat swayed easily nearby.

As in a dream, he heard a human voice. Lindall opened his eyes and listened. No, he had not imagined it. Someone was shouting right into his ears.

"Well, where are you going, silly? Where are you going, silly, silly?"

His heart thumped and stopped.

"Where are you going, silly?" came from the earphones. Lindall swam rapidly to the boat. The blood hammered in his temples. He caught at the side of the boat and, at the risk of capsizing it, rolled over into the bottom. He could not have swum faster if he had been pursued by a tiger shark.

"Where are you going, silly?" the words continued in his ears. With a sharp movement, Lindall switched the earphones from ultrasonic to normal range.

Everything was silent. Only the omnipresent alpheus lobsters and the hermit crabs crunched, chewing seashells.

"So I'm not out of my mind," Lindall said to himself, and switched on the ultrasonic wavelength once again. And again he heard, even more distinctly:

> "Fierce air and violent light,
> sail rent and sundering oar,
> Darkness and noises of night . . ."

"What the devil?" he wondered. The fear was gone now. But his body still retained the memory of the first moment of panic, which had driven him, with wide, staring eyes, to fling himself into the boat. He was trembling, and his tanned skin was covered with gooseflesh despite the hot sun.

"Clamor of currents and foam," the sound roared in his earphones. "Good-bye, silly. Where are you going, silly? Come back to take out the stitches! . . ."

"Oh, no!" cried Lindall. " 'Come back to take out the stitches'? But that's what I said to the dolphin in parting. And the poem is mine!"

"The poem is mine," echoed the earphones.

Lindall pulled off his helmet and removed the earphones. A fragrant silence surrounded him. The melodic plashing of the sea made the silence still deeper. He looked around him. A dolphin was playing in the waves about a hundred yards from the boat. He swam in circles. Gathering speed, he left behind him a deep furrow in the water; then he leaped up into the air and splashed triumphantly back. Crystal fountains rose into the rich blue sky, like gleaming salutes to the sun.

Lindall still could not calm down. He put on the earphones and immediately heard:

"The poem is mine! Where are you going, silly?"

He pulled off the earphones and heard the dolphin swishing through the water.

"Is that you speaking?" asked Lindall.

The dolphin was silent. He continued to circle busily near the boat, leaping from the waves.

"If not you, then who?" asked Lindall again. "Could I be speaking to myself?"

He noticed that he had the earphones in his hand and put them on again. And once again he heard human speech:

"Where are you going, silly? Wailing of waves on the shore. Is that you speaking? Come back to take out the stitches!"

"Oh-h, so it is you!" Lindall sighed in relief. "Well, nothing special, really. Just a talking dolphin. I speak and he repeats."

"A talking dolphin. A talking dolphin. Where are you going, silly?" the earphones replied.

This was the first contact between them.

It did not take Lindall long to teach the dolphin to come when he was called. Now I'm a real Robinson Crusoe, he thought. I have my parrot. All I need is to teach him to say tearfully, "Poor Percival Lindall," and everything will be just right. But then, I must name him, too. A pity I don't remember the name of Robinson's parrot. . . .

Lindall named the dolphin Kidd. He celebrated by treating Kidd to a fat whiting, and the dolphin began to accompany him on all his journeys. Whenever Lindall, for one reason or another, stayed on the island, Kidd would swim as close to the shore as he could and wait for him, rocking in the waves.

At times it seemed to Lindall that the dolphin understood human speech instead of mechanically remembering words and phrases. Kidd's answers were sometimes so apt that Lindall wondered. . . .

From the day when the dolphin acquired a human voice, Lindall ceased studying the voices of the sea. It became impossible. Kidd interfered by constant chattering. The moment Lindall switched on the hydrophone to ultrasonic range, he was overwhelmed by a veritable avalanche of words, an endless mixture of exclamations, interjections, marine terms, and verse. At first Lindall tried to outwit the dolphin. He would row away windward and silently begin his investigations. But, by some infallible instinct, Kidd always found the man. Lindall would hear him before he appeared. "Percival, Percival!" the call would come muted by distance, and, annoyed though he was, Lindall felt pleased at the animal's devotion.

One day he taught Kidd the dialogue between Cassio and Iago, assigning the more difficult role of Iago to the dolphin. Another day the dolphin repaid the man for rescuing him. He saved the man's life.

Lindall had long noticed a large octopus that lived in a deep grotto under the northernmost cape. The desire to catch him became an obsession. Mentally, Lindall anticipated the delicious meals he would prepare—black soup à la Sparta from the head, a delicate dish of the tentacles, roasted over a slow fire.

A tongue of lava overhung the grotto like a huge balcony, and it was impossible to reach the grotto from the shore. The only approach was from the sea. Lindall rowed for a long time against a strong current that circled the spot, until he finally came to the dark niche, overgrown with polyps and mollusks. He waited until his eyes became accustomed to the dark, anchored the boat, took a fish-spear and dived in. The depth of the water was not more than thirty feet, but the cold springs rising from the bottom kept the temperature so low that it was impossible to remain submerged for long.

Orange ascidias were delicately opalescent in the dusk of the grotto. Shrimps gleamed like greenish points of light. A spiny lobster crawled up the seaweed-covered rock, waving its long yellow and blue antennae. The octopus was not there. He must have gone out somewhere on business of his own. Lindall speared the lobster, glanced around him, and swam toward the entrance.

Two dark shadows floated slowly past the grotto, with

fins spread wide, like bomber planes in the evening sky.

Lindall felt that the reserves of air in his lungs were almost exhausted. To relieve the sense of suffocation, he began to let bubbles escape from his mouth. They rose, glinting like nickel pellets. But this was only a momentary delay. It was necessary to rise to the surface, and Lindall knew that the instant he swam out, the blue sharks would attack his legs. Seconds congealed into ages. The gray bombers, showing no aggressive intentions, were circling patiently at the entrance to the grotto. It seemed to Lindall that his head was bursting with red fire. Everything turned dark before his eyes. He expelled all the air from his lungs and, no longer conscious of anything, his belly drawn in, he feverishly started working with his arms. His head shot out of the water like a cork. Without opening his eyes, Lindall gulped the sharp, intoxicating air. His head reeled, and a blessed sense of well-being spread throughout his body. He had forgotten all about the sharks and his unprotected legs.

When Lindall finally looked down into the cold, dark-blue depths, he cried out with surprise. Directly before him he saw a madly circling wheel, and some distance away, two motionless, baffled sharks. Lindall rapidly swam to the boat, grasped the stern, and, with a sharp flip of the fins, rolled over into the hot, dry bottom. Kidd leaped from the water, spun around and around on a horizontal axis, and dashed away into the open sea, leaving behind him a faint, foamy trace. Lindall tore off his mask and turned over on his face to warm his back. He relished the air, breathing it in noisily and deeply. In the dark waters of the niche, a pair of slanting fins slid back and forth like sails. Lindall took up the oars and rowed farther out into the sunlight.

The tropical sun stood at the zenith. The air was fiery with midday heat. Something stirred in the boat, and Lindall discovered, to his astonishment, the lobster, huddled in a tiny, rapidly evaporating puddle. So he hadn't abandoned his quarry! He laughed.

In order to keep track of time, Lindall drew a calendar for several years in advance and marked off every passing day. It was already the third year of his solitude when he heard again the hum of airplane motors in the night sky. The planes disappeared before he managed to build a fire. Lindall was in despair. He did not go out in his boat for a whole week, and Kidd waited for him vainly near the shore. After that night, though, the planes came more and more often, and Lindall succeeded three times in making fires just when the squadrons were above the island.

Nevertheless, the fliers did not seem to have noticed his signals. Lindall fought down attacks of panic. He realized that even in the omnipotent twentieth century a man could rot alive on an uninhabited island. He began to consider a journey to some neighboring islands, and even started to make a sail out of the tarpaulin with which he had covered his supplies. The crates of foodstuffs had long been emptied, and he lived by hunting and fishing.

One day he wandered in search of quarry to the eastern rim of the island, marveling, as he always did, at the sharp changes of landscape. After a half-hour's walk through the woods, he came to an open, rocky plateau that broke off steeply toward the water. There, among the black cliffs polished by the tides, was one of the world's last great colonies of marine iguanas.

During the ebb tide the giant lizards climbed down from the rocks to eat a favorite food—the seaweed left behind by the receding water. Lindall was in luck. He found the animals in their mating season, when the males become extremely aggressive.

The rookery was reminiscent of a vast gladiators' arena. As a rule, the males select small platforms where they settle with several females. If a rival approaches the chosen spot, the master assumes a threatening pose and tries to scare him off. He raises his spiny crest, opens his fiery red maw, and circles around and around on the same spot, rhythmically shaking his head. If the uninvited guest persists, a duel follows.

Hiding behind a large rock overgrown with golden lichen, Lindall watched two males about to start a fight. With bowed heads, the rivals rushed at each other, bumped heads, and halted tensely. This lasted some seven minutes, until the newcomer yielded and placed himself at the mercy of the victor. He flattened himself submissively and stayed motionless in this humble pose. The victor did not even deign to touch his prostrate foe. Proud and still menacing, he waited for the vanquished iguana to crawl away.

Concentrating on the iguanas, Lindall never once glanced at the sea, or he would have discerned a tiny spot on the horizon. It was a bluish-gray torpedo boat, with an American flag, steaming full speed toward the island.

One of Lindall's signals, it turned out, had been noticed by the pilot of a night bomber based on a newly built airfield on the island of Baltra. The commander of the base became alarmed, thinking that the uninhabited island might harbor Japanese spies, and sent out a torpedo boat to reconnoiter.

When Lindall, crazed with joy, was embracing the Americans and piling his collections and his few belongings into the waiting launch, he never for a moment thought of Kidd. Not that he had forgotten him—he simply did not think of him. And only when the motors started in the torpedo boat and Lindall threw a last glance at his island did he suddenly remember Kidd. He was standing on deck, talking to a young marine corporal. The corporal squatted, embracing his tommy gun with both arms, and showered Lindall with questions. He wanted to know everything—what Lindall ate, when his supply of whisky ran out, how he managed living alone.

The thought of Kidd stung Lindall with sharp pain. He was ready to rush to the captain and plead with him to put off the departure, or else jump overboard and swim back to the island.

"Kidd! Kidd! Kidd!" he shouted, folding his hands like a trumpet.

And the dolphin heard him. The anchor had barely been lifted when Lindall caught sight of him. He did not swim—he flew in answer to the call. A few feet from the ship, the animal leaped up into the air. Lindall stretched his arms to him, as though to embrace him, as though to tell him something. The gun barked sharply at his ear. Without completing his beautiful parabola, the dolphin dropped like a stone into the water and disappeared under the waves, leaving a stream of red bubbles on the surface.

"Just right! Just as he leaped!" cried the corporal.

With a hoarse shout, Lindall threw himself at the corporal and knocked him off his feet. In a frenzy, in utter silence, he banged the man's head over and over on the boards of the deck. He never knew when he was pulled away from the unconscious American. He never felt it when he was kicked again and again, then thrown into a dark hole under the ship's kitchen.

Lindall was sure the American had killed Kidd, or he would have returned to the island. No one expected him in England. His *Galápagos* had been found, overturned, on the Florida coast, and everyone assumed that Lindall had perished. His parents were dead. His wife was about to remarry.

Yes, if Lindall knew that Kidd recovered from the wound, he would have gone back. But he did not know. He joined the air force and bombed Nazi ships. In 1943 he was shot down over Normandy.

But Kidd survived. And waited for Lindall's return. You may smile, but I am certain that he never stopped waiting.

After the Americans had built their base on Baltra, the Tortoise Islands ceased to be forgotten spots of primeval peace. Ships and tourists came to visit them. They came to Lindall's island as well. And every time a ship approached the line of underwater reefs, a dolphin swam up to it and guided it safely through the only open passage to where the travelers could see a wide, shingled beach. This was why the sailors nicknamed him "pilot."

And Kidd? Surely, he expected Lindall to return. Speak to any acoustician of the ships plying the routes along the coast of Central and South America. They can tell you a good deal. As soon as any dolphins appear in the vicinity of a ship, the hydrophones pick up their calls. And what do you think they cry?

"Percival! Percival!" This is the cry of all the dolphins in that part of the Pacific. You understand? All of them.

VICTOR KOLUPAYEV

A Ticket to Childhood

"A ticket to childhood, please," I said to the man behind the window. Five minutes later I sat in a hard seat in an old-fashioned railway car and waited impatiently for the locomotive whistle.

Next to me was an old woman with a basket of fruit and candy. The excitement with which she kept arranging and rearranging the contents of the basket might have seemed comical elsewhere, but not on this train. It was easy to understand her feelings. After all, she was going to visit a little girl, the girl she had been many years ago, and she had probably long forgotten what it was like to be a child. All she knew was that children are fond of sweets, and she was bringing them into her own childhood.

Across the way from me sat a man with graying temples and an old man. I knew the younger man from pictures in the newspapers. He was a famous pianist. Before every concert he took a trip to childhood. People said that this was why his concerts were so extraordinary. I doubt it, though. Many musicians visited their childhood, but the journey did not turn anybody else into a genius.

The old man sat resting his hands on the handle of a massive cane. All he was taking as a gift to his childhood was the wise look in his tired eyes.

The train started. Telegraph poles flashed by, the wheels clicked rhythmically, from time to time the locomotive let out a long, slow whistle. Somebody in the next car asked the conductor for cold beer, then grumbled for a long time about the poor service.

An hour passed. Everyone was sad and pensive. Beyond the turn appeared a platform.

"We're here," said the conductor.

The passengers rose hastily and crowded toward the door.

"Suzdal!" my neighbor exclaimed with astonishment.

It was Zagorsk. To me it was Zagorsk. And to her, Suzdal. To the old man, Penza or Syzran. Everyone arrived in the city of his childhood. I looked at the walls of the ancient monastery. Someone else looked out on the taiga, the swift current of the Yenisey River, the lazy ripples of Lake Onega.

Zagorsk. . . . And I had not even known that this was my city. I did not remember my childhood.

The old woman saw a plump little girl in the crowd that came to meet the train. She waved her handkerchief and started crying. The pianist put his hand on the shoulder of a little boy, and they walked toward the viaduct, earnest and deep in thought. The platform was crowded and noisy, but little by little the people dispersed.

No one came to meet me. Several times I waved to little boys, but someone else would approach them. Every time it wasn't I. It was difficult for me to imagine what I was like in childhood, particularly since I did not have a single photograph of that time. And, generally, I doubted whether I had ever been photographed as a child.

Within ten minutes there was no one near the train except a ten-year-old boy in a T-shirt and disproportionately large pants, who was poking an empty ice-cream container with his worn shoe.

"Sashka!" I cried. But he did not even glance at me. He jumped down from the platform, crossed the rails, and disappeared around the corner of a building.

Trying to search for myself in the city was senseless. I lingered aimlessly at the station for about an hour, waiting for the train to start on the return trip.

All the way back to Ust-Mansk I was filled with a sense of irreparable loss. Why didn't he come? Why? My neighbors in the car were sunk in their own thoughts, and only one woman tried to tell anyone who would listen about her pranks of forty years ago, but nobody would listen.

As I came off the train at the Ust-Mansk station, I was called to the dispatcher.

"Forgive us, please," said a young man in a railway uniform when I entered the office and identified myself. "We spoiled your trip, it's our fault. Something must have gone wrong with the time field system. Or it might be that our tempogram did not reach the addressee, and so he did not come to meet you."

"Perhaps he did not want to meet me," I said and turned to leave.

"It won't happen again," the dispatcher assured me. "We'll make sure to check everything. You can take another trip to childhood, tomorrow if you wish."

"I doubt that I'll have time this month." I turned and left without saying good-by.

I was setting up an important experiment, and I was

really short of time. Nevertheless, the next day I was again at the station, I traveled again in the dilapidated car, and stood again on the emptying platform.

At the end of the platform I saw the same boy.

"Sashka," I cried. "It *is* you!" I felt it, I knew it beyond question.

He wanted to jump down, but changed his mind and remained standing, looking down at his feet. I rushed toward him, seized him by the shoulders, and pressed him to my chest. And suddenly, he clung to me. For a second, no longer. Then he drew away and, looking at me from under his brow, he said:

"So that's what you're like!" And something unchildlike, grown up, was in his voice. Generally, he was much too serious for his age.

"Sashka! So you did recognize me?"

"Of course I did. But I'm not Sashka. Everybody calls me Roland. Well, Rolka."

"But my name is Alexander. So you must be Sashka."

He shrugged.

At the age of forty, I am a strong, muscular man. And he was awkward and skinny.

"Listen, Sashka, I'll call you Alexander, not Roland."

He shrugged again, as if to say, "As you wish."

"Why are you so skinny, you imp?" I asked. "You must take up sports, or you won't last long."

For a moment it seemed to me that his eyes were laughing at me, and I burst out laughing, too. What nonsense I was talking. Here I was before him, alive and well. So how could he not "last long"? Ridiculous.

We laughed as we walked to the viaduct, slapping one another on the back, unable to speak through the laughter.

The station square was different from the one I knew from my visits to Zagorsk. I usually dined at the Astra restaurant, but there was no trace of it here. From the right came the hubbub of a marketplace, which even the locomotive whistles did not drown out.

"All right, Sashka," I said. "I know it's difficult to act right off in a way that won't seem funny to one of us. I'm sure I'll say more silly things. But that shouldn't prevent us from having a good dinner somewhere."

"I'm not hungry," said Sashka. "We've had our dinner."

What was going on within him, really? I tried to put myself in his place. If I were hungry, I'd never refuse an invitation from someone like myself. But then, I am an adult. . . .

"Well, if you'd rather not. . . ." I said. "But tell me where you live, tell me about your friends."

"No, please. No questions," he answered, and I realized that I must have sounded to him like a dry, official interrogator who could not be answered frankly and sincerely.

We approached the little market square, and I asked:

"How about some ice cream?"

"Um-m," he answered eagerly.

"With fruit, or nuts?"

"Who ever heard of that?"

"Let's see," I said mysteriously. But the ice-cream vendor really had neither. I asked, just to make sure, but I should have kept quiet. She suddenly turned upon me. "Look at him!" she scolded. "What will you want next?" Sashka tugged at my sleeve.

"Let's go. . . ."

All the same, I bought a portion of ordinary ice cream. Sashka accepted it, looking aside, and I had to tell him twice to eat it before he unwrapped the package. And immediately, it seemed to me, he had forgotten all about my presence. I realized, with a pang, how much he wanted that ice cream. An ordinary ten-year-old, whose dreams and desires don't go beyond such small things. Some of the ice cream dripped on his absurdly wide pants, and he wiped them at once with his elbow.

"Have you learned to heal incurable sicknesses?" he suddenly asked me.

I was taken aback.

"How do you know?" After all, I started working on the problem when I was about twenty-five, and drifted into it quite by chance.

"But I am you," he said. "Only in your childhood. I know more about you than you about me, because I always wanted you to be like me and do the things I wanted to do. I want it very much."

Childish naivete and adult seriousness were strangely combined in him.

"No, Sashka, I have not learned yet to cure incurable diseases. But I think it won't be long now before it becomes possible."

"Really?" he cried joyfully.

"Really." I patted him on the head. "But I never have enough time. You're lucky. You don't yet notice how fast time flies."

He threw me a strange glance, slightly mocking, as if he knew something very important to me, but did not yet consider it necessary to tell me about it. His faded trousers were baggy, his checkered shirt had lost its colors. Life isn't very kind to you, I thought.

"I haven't enough time, either," he said at last.

"Indeed?" I smiled. "And what is it you do that leaves you no time?"

"I want you to come out happy. . . ."

"Oh, well. Consider that I have come out happy. But do you know what happiness is?"

He did not answer, as though he had not heard the question.

"I also want people to be happier because you exist."

Well, that was something I couldn't be sure of. Are people happier because I exist? No, I could not answer this with certainty.

"You're terribly serious, Sashka. That's not so good at your age, you know."

"It's good."

"All right, we won't argue. But tell me, why didn't you come up to me yesterday?"

"You did not come to me at once, either. Why should I have rushed to you right away? I waited for you, too."

"Forgive me."

It seemed to me that there was suddenly a wall of alienation between us, that we were strangers, and that I would never come to understand this ten-year-old boy, either because adults never understand children, or because he was more intelligent than I. But I discarded the second supposition at once; I could not admit the possibility that I was growing more foolish with age. At any rate, this had never occurred to me before I met him.

We wandered through the city for a long time. I learned that he did not remember his parents either; they had evidently been killed during the war, and he was living in an orphanage. I thought that he was so reticent and secretive because this was our first meeting. It is difficult to say much or to talk lightly when you come face to face with yourself for the first time.

Later I realized that, although he spoke less, it was he who directed the conversation. He seemed to put me through an examination, but he did it imperceptibly, without insistence. And I was compelled to admit that he was, after all, in some indefinable way more intelligent than I. Perhaps it was his manner of thinking, his ability to know exactly what he wanted, his astonishing self-possession and irony. A sad irony, strangely at odds with his age.

We agreed to meet again. I left by the evening train. At the very last moment, when I was already in the car, he laughed gaily, jumped up and down several times, and cried to me:

"You're all right! Not quite what I supposed, but all right, anyway. So long!"

The sense of alienation was suddenly gone. And again it was his doing.

"So long, Sashka!" I called out.

The train started. I was filled with joy—so much joy I could barely contain it.

And yet I did not know, could not imagine, how necessary this meeting had been to me. I began to work as I had not worked in a very long time. A burst of inspiration took possession of me. Now I was sure that the experiment would succeed. I would achieve what I had evidently dreamed about when I was still a child.

Several months flew by, unnoticed. Successes, great and small, sleepless nights, fleeting doubts, heated debates and discussions, meetings with other scientists, trips. Our institute was working on a vital and difficult problem. We sought to develop instantaneous nonsurgical methods of treating injuries at a distance. Let us say a man fell off a cliff and was badly hurt. By the time he could be brought to a hospital, it would be too late. We were devising methods and apparatus that would transform the bag of pain and broken bones back into a sound human being, so that a man who fell off a cliff would get up at once, whole and unharmed.

We wanted to diminish the number of unnecessary deaths. And we were succeeding. Now I could say, "Yes, people will be happier because I exist." Say it to Sashka, that is, to myself, and to no one else.

It was only after six months that I could find the time and buy another ticket to childhood. . . . Sashka did not come to the station.

Childish, ridiculous behavior, I thought. He is probably offended because it has taken me so long to come. And I can now tell him so much about the things he dreamed of!

Badly upset, I returned to Ust-Mansk. At the station, I was again invited to the dispatcher's office.

"Did anything go wrong with the tempogram?" I asked hopefully.

"No, we sent the tempogram. But the trouble is. . . . Well, you see, you did not have a childhood. . . . It seems incredible, but it is so."

"What nonsense! I saw. . . . I have already spoken to Sashka."

"It was not Sashka. I mean, it wasn't you as a child. It was Roland Yevstafiev."

Roland Yevstafiev? I'd never known anyone by that name. Yet it seemed oddly familiar.

"You had no childhood."

"But why, then, did he come to meet me? No! Of course, it's he, I mean, I. I feel it, I'm sure of it."

"You had no childhood. It's an unusual case."

They brought me a glass of water. I must have looked distraught and pitiful. I dropped into a chair, unable to go out into the street. They left me alone and did not speak to me again. What could they say? They had discovered that I never had a childhood. Why and how? They did not know. And they could not help me in any way.

When a man has had a difficult or unhappy childhood, it is said that he did not have a childhood. But I! I had no childhood in the most direct, literal sense.

After a while, I recovered a little. At least enough to walk in the street without drawing the attention of passersby.

An hour later I was in my laboratory. It was quite late, and only two or three people were still there. I sat down at my desk and tried to collect my thoughts. Soon the laboratory was empty. My colleagues may have spoken to me before leaving. I heard nothing. . . . The only sound was the chattering of a typewriter in the next room. It was Yelena Dmitrievna, typing up the records of our experiments.

I sat at the desk, straining to remember. I searched my memory for facts, I put them together, I compared and tried to find some meaning in them.

Fifteen years before, I had been ill for a long time. During that illness I lost my memory. I had no recollection of my friends, my acquaintances, or myself before the illness. It was strange—the only thing that remained clear in my mind was the sum of knowledge and experience of a young scientist on the threshold of his career. All personal memories, everything connected with my own life had disappeared. I was like a man freshly reborn. A young woman, Lena Yevstafieva, often came to visit me. Yelena Dmitrievna Yevstafieva. She had been working for many years now as my secretary. One evening, about a year after my illness, she suddenly burst out crying at her desk. I raised her tear-stained face.

"You aren't like. . . . You're altogether different," she said.

"Not like what?" I asked foolishly.

She got up and went out. It was the only time she left the institute before me. When I questioned her afterward, she said:

"Don't ask. Nothing happened."

And I never asked. Almost as if I was afraid of hearing something. . . . What? I did not know.

I dialed the records department and asked for a list of people who worked at the institute fifteen years before. At that time it had been only a small laboratory. A monotonous voice read off a list of names: Abramov, Volkov, Roland Yevstafiev. . . .

Wait! So he worked here, too. I tried to recall. No, I did not remember him.

Looking through the files, I learned that Roland Yevstafiev died on the day I lost my memory. Lost my memory?

Suddenly I understood. I never lost my memory. I simply did not exist. I began my . . . existence on the day he died.

Who was I, then? A cyborg—an artificial, cybernetic organism? Who ever heard of a cyborg who has had his appendix removed and who frequently caught colds? No.

His consciousness, his "I" was programmed in my body? No.

He created me and died. This had nothing to do with my body, or even my brain cells. He created me in some different, much more complex sense. He created my manner of thinking, my intellect. And I must be what he had wanted me to be.

And that boy? So he had thought it all out—he had known it already, at the age of ten, and that was why he spoke to me so strangely. Already, then, he knew that I was what he would create in the future, because he would not have time enough himself to complete his work.

I was not meant to be. I had not been planned in the rosters of nature. But here I was. I had no childhood. He gave me a little piece of his own. I didn't know how he made this incredible discovery. No one knew. . . . No one?

The telephone rang in the next room. Yelena Dmitrievna picked up the receiver.

That ten-year-old boy did everything for me, and asked nothing in return. Nothing, except a portion of plain ice cream.

And he wanted to see me only once, to see whether he would do the right thing one day in the future.

I can hear Yelena Dmitrievna, Lena, getting up from her chair. She is coming toward my laboratory in her light, graceful walk.

In a moment she will open the door, and I will ask her everything. I will ask her who I am.

And she will tell me.

The door is opening.

In a moment, I'll learn everything. . . .

GENNADY GOR

THE GARDEN

[ONE]

"Arden," said Nina, "did the sociologist ask how you came into our century?"

"He did."

"And you told him?"

"I did."

"Did he believe you?"

"I don't know. When I answered his questionnaire, I wrote the word 'Future' with a capital letter. At first he thought that there's a village called Future, somewhere on the edge of the Antarctic, and that I was born there. But I explained it to him."

"Arden, how can it be explained? Don't you know that sociologists accept nothing but facts?"

"But this is also a fact."

"An odd fact. A man is born in the twenty-first century, but somehow gets into the twentieth. And the sociologist did not ask you for proof?"

"For the time being, no. But he will come again. He is looking for the general and typical, for something subject to statistical laws. And here he stumbled on such an extraordinary case. I thought he'd explode. He looked at me as if I were a madman. Then he tore up the questionnaire. Then he calmed down and we had a talk. He asked whether my answer was metaphorical, and I said, 'No, I was really born in the twenty-first century. It's no metaphor.' Then he said that this was a purely philosophical answer, and a metaphor all the same. What amazed me, though, was that he really believed me in the end."

"He did? I think he just pretended. A scientist isn't likely to believe a thing that is against all logic."

"But Nina, he turned out to be very trusting. At first he doubted me, then he became convinced. I answered all his questions about the twenty-first century. He seemed to be most interested in what people will drink in the twenty-first century—tea or coffee. I said coffee. And he felt better at once. But let's forget him now. We'll talk about him when I finish my work."

Arden was sketching a silhouette of a tree on a large sheet of drawing paper, and Nina sat in a rocking chair with a slender book in her hand, reading poetry. From time to time she glanced at the poet's photograph on the back of the jacket. The poet looked like Arden. So much like him that it gave Nina a queer feeling. But he could not be Arden, and Arden could not be him. The poet was born two centuries before Arden.

"Arden," said Nina, "I woke up last night and you weren't there. Where were you?"

"Outside the window."

"What were you doing there?"

"Nothing. Just standing."

"Why?"

"Haven't I told you many times that at night I turn into a garden? They taught me there how to do it."

"Where?"

"In the future."

"In the village called Future?"

"No, in the future that will come."

"A man can turn into a garden only in a fairy tale. And

what's around us is not a fairy tale. I hope you didn't tell the sociologist that you turn into a garden at night?"

"I told him."

"What for?"

"He wanted to know what I feel when I paint my pictures. He wanted to know everything: what I feel, what I experience, what I think. The sociologist was very anxious to get inside my soul. And I let him in."

Nina laughed.

"You let him in, but you won't let me in. We've lived together for half a year now, and I still don't know anything about your past."

"My past is the future. I am living not from the beginning, but from the end. I've never concealed this from you. The date in my passport confuses everyone."

"A mistake of the passport office?"

"No, a slight inaccuracy. They wrote the year 2000, and I was born in 2003, twenty-eight years from now. I hurried, Nina, and came into the world without waiting for the date that was assigned to me by chance. You see, in the world I came from, chance has been abolished. There, people don't get born by chance."

[TWO]

Nina first met Arden in the city garden. She sat on a bench, with her book beside her, unread, and listened to the rustling of the trees. It was quite windy. And the garden rustled over her head. Suddenly it was silent. This was very strange, it was inexplicable. The wind was as strong as before. But the branches no longer waved, and did not rustle. The trees were still, like a reflection in a pool.

Nina heard steps. A young man stopped before her. He held a branch of cherry blossoms in his hand.

"You're not allowed to break branches here," said Nina sternly. "Who are you?"

"Who am I now?" asked the young man. "Or who was I five minutes ago?"

"Have you managed to change in five minutes?"

"Yes, I have. I was in a great hurry. I wanted to meet you. I often see you here with a book."

"Why, then, have I never seen you before?"

"Of course, you've seen me, but you didn't guess it was I. I didn't look like myself."

"And how did you look?"

"Oh. . . . But you won't believe me anyway."

"Why not? You have such an honest face, you couldn't be a liar. Do tell me how you looked."

"Later," the young man said with a slight frown. "The important thing is not how I looked half an hour ago, but how I look now."

"Now you look like a person who has just passed a difficult test."

"You guessed it. I've really just passed a test. I've turned into a human being again."

"And what were you before?"

"I was a garden," he answered softly.

"What?"

"A garden."

"A garden? I'm afraid I don't understand you. A garden cannot turn into a man."

"It can. But I wasn't always a garden, only sometimes, when I wanted it very much."

"You were turned into a garden by an evil sorcerer?"

"No, not an evil one. I'd say a good one. But that's a secret. And I have no right to reveal it. I signed a promise."

"Promise to whom?"

"To the director of the Institute of Sorcery and Fairy Tales."

"And where is this institute?"

"It does not exist as yet. But it will. I too should not exist yet, but I hurried, and now I'm here. I could not allow chance to divide us. I've come here from a century that is yet to be. In order to see you every day, I turned myself into a garden. I have stood here in rain, in storms, in heat and cold, waiting for you."

"Are you slightly mad? Or making fun of me? You speak of things that are impossible."

"Impossible to you. Possible to me. At the Institute of Sorcery and Fairy Tales they've found a way of turning people into natural phenomena, as in ancient myths. Besides, I am an artist, and it helps me in my work. I seldom paint people. I do landscapes. There will be an exhibition of my paintings at the Russian Museum. I'll send you a ticket for the opening."

[THREE]

He sent her an invitation. It was printed in red and black, and it said, "The Leningrad Section of the Artists' Union and the Russian State Museum invite you to the opening of the exhibition of works by Arden Nikolayevich Cloudin."

So he has a name, she thought, and a patronymic, and a family name. Cloudin. It suits him. And he's a member of the Artists' Union too. But, then, what is so amazing about that? As if it were perfectly all right for an ordinary person to turn into a garden, but not for a member of the Artists' Union.

Nina examined the ticket with wonder. Paintings, draw-ings, engravings, illustrations. So he illustrates children's books! The editors probably don't know that he can turn into a garden. If they knew, they wouldn't be likely to trust him with children's books.

Nina went to the museum. It was very crowded. The exhibition was opened by a gray-haired, dignified art historian. He spoke distinctly and weightily:

"Arden Nikolayevich Cloudin, despite his youth, has already managed to bring a new element into the art of painting. His watercolors are enchanting, as though the paper had absorbed into itself the blue of the sky, the glow of clouds, the freshness of morning dew. . . ."

Cloudin stood next to the critic. Now it was easy to believe that he had come from another age. He stood there, ready to vanish, looking out of the corner of his eye at a statue behind which he apparently longed to hide from all that praise.

Nina smiled to him, but he did not see her. There were too many people between them. A pretty girl, a museum employee, handed the venerable art historian a pair of scissors. He awkwardly cut the ribbon, and the crowd, together with Nina, flowed into the exhibition hall.

Stopping at the first watercolor, Nina saw her own image behind the glass. Not even her image—her own self, but on paper and under glass, and ten or even twenty times smaller.

Nina saw herself with Cloudin's eyes. He painted pure transparent colors on the sheet of paper, and her face shone through as if reflected in a stream. The clear, fresh water washed her image, cleansing it of everything ordinary, casual. In the painting she was a part of nature, of woods, lakes, clouds mirrored in the water.

Suddenly she heard his voice:

"You are here! I am so glad you came."

Arden was standing next to her.

"You're Cloudin?" Nina said. "I did not know you had a name, and even a family name."

He smiled.

"Of course. A garden cannot have a family name. A garden is a part of nature, and human names are too confining for nature. But the Artists' Union does not admit people without names. And so I had to go to the police and get a passport. Besides, being a garden is only my second profession. A garden and an artist—they're almost colleagues."

"Why do you pretend you are a garden? It's so absurd."

"I don't pretend I am a garden. It is the garden that pretends it's I. But when you came, I turned into a man."

"You speak so strangely. When I was a child, fairy tales spoke to me like that."

"Your childhood has returned to you. And you have come into a fairy-tale world. A world where there are no mental barriers between things, phenomena, and humans. A world that has become more fluid. But we'll talk about it later. I want you to see my landscapes."

Making a way through the crowd, he led her to his landscapes. Everybody recognized him. She heard one artist speak to another behind them:

"He studied in Paris with Matisse himself."

"How could he have studied with Matisse? Matisse has long been dead."

"Look at the catalogue. The introduction says that he is a student of Matisse."

Nina asked Cloudin:

"You studied with Matisse?"

"Yes," he answered quietly.

"But Matisse died before you were born."

"Before, after, that's not important. I was born in the future and I'm here, in your century. I visited Matisse, too. I made myself into a garden under his window. He painted me. We were friends."

"Why do you speak so strangely?"

"I speak the truth. The truth may be difficult to fit into the logic of life, but not into the logic of the fairy tale. And didn't we agree we are in a fairy tale? There is a fairy-tale relationship between us. But now, look at this landscape. It is called 'The Garden.' Do you recognize it?"

She turned her eyes to it and knew it at once. It was the garden where they met. But it was at the same time both a garden and a man, as in Ovid's *Metamorphoses*. The young man in the picture was a part of nature. He had not quite separated himself from it as yet. The colors were as fresh as morning, as the ripples on the blue surface of a pond. The painting looked like music, transformed into pure, unmixed colors pressed directly from the tubes onto the paper. Or no, not from tubes, but from branches and grasses, from the dawn. The living, delicate hues of the garden were captured on the paper, as if the garden itself were here, with the wind, with the morning.

"This watercolor," he said quietly, "pleased Matisse."

"Matisse died twenty years ago."

"I lived then, too."

"And worked with him? How could you? You look no older than twenty-five."

"That's unimportant. I can be younger and older than myself. Sometimes I can do it, at other times I can't. Then I feel I am untalented. But here's a critic pushing his way toward us. From the expression on his face, I expect nothing good."

Nina stepped aside. From time to time she glanced around. The critic's puffy face turned gloomier and gloomier as he talked in an undertone to Arden.

Nina looked at a watercolor: a wide window, thrown open into spring, into the woods. It seemed that somewhere near the window, in the woods, an oriole was whistling, trilling fluidly. The artist had caught in colors something inexpressible in color—a bird's song. Then a cuckoo started up, and the wood absorbed the sounds and returned them again.

Nina listened. She now heard the critic's grumbling voice:

"These are sketches, not paintings. You can't substitute colors for subjects. You don't know how to paint. Matisse hasn't taught you anything!"

[FOUR]

At the marriage registry office, the clerk asked:

"When were you born, Arden Nikolayevich?"

"In the year 2003."

The clerk laughed.

"Before Christ?"

"No, after."

"But now it is only 1975."

"If you don't believe me, see my passport."

The young man opened the passport and his face darkened.

"I will record your marriage, Mr. Cloudin, but you must get your passport corrected. It's an obvious mistake. You couldn't have been born in a century that is still in the future."

"I could."

"Let's not argue. This is a government office."

What would the sober young man have said if he had learned that there was no mistake, and that Arden Cloudin was really decades younger than himself? But neither Arden nor Nina took the trouble to explain to him a fact that could not be explained. They received their marriage certificate and went home.

The taxi driver listened to a conversation that made no sense to him, and became more and more nervous. The words were familiar, but he did not understand them, and he almost got into an accident. The taxi driver liked everything to be orderly and sensible.

"I've almost begun to believe," said Nina, "that you were really born in 2003. But how did you get here from the future?"

"Nina, you pose the question incorrectly. The important thing is not how, but what for. I came into the past to meet you. I could not accept the accident of your having been born fifty years before me. I found your picture in my grandmother's old family album, and I did everything I could to meet you. Well, I've succeeded."

"But. . . ."

"Again you want to ask me how. And again the question is wrong. How can Pushkin or Shakespeare talk to us? They can, because people have invented a way of bringing distant generations together, of making them contemporary. This invention is called writing. It is imperfect, though. Pushkin can talk to us, but we can't talk to him. In the Institute of Sorcery and Fairy Tales where I worked, we found a way of talking to Pushkin and Shakespeare, not across centuries, but directly, as I talk to you now. But I am living at the same time in my own century as well."

"Can't you explain it to me?"

"Another wrong question. In order to answer it, I'd have to recall what is not yet, but is still to come. And then it would not be recollection, but a dream. Do you want me to dream?"

"I do," said Nina. "I love to see you dreaming."

The taxi driver pulled up to the curb and stopped abruptly.

"Get out," he said.

"Are we there?" asked Nina with surprise.

"Doesn't matter. Get out. I won't take you any farther."

"Did you run out of gasoline?"

"I've all the gasoline I want. Get out. Dream somewhere else, not in my cab. I can't stand dreamers. Excuse me, I must get to the taxi stand near the Gorky subway."

[FIVE]

They settled in Nina's room. After all, they couldn't live in the garden, under the open sky, where Cloudin said he had stood waiting for Nina.

He had no place of his own; he was waiting for the Artists' Union to get him an apartment. But he was seventh in a long list, and his turn hadn't come.

True, he had an excellent sunny studio where he both worked and lived—during those hours, naturally, when he was a man and not a garden.

He was appointed a member of a commission to select paintings for a spring exhibition, and he disqualified a monumental canvas by a certain venerable and highly influential man. Nothing changed after that, except the waiting list for apartments. Arden suddenly found himself in the seventeenth rather than the seventh place. To tell the truth, he was not too upset about it. He had left an excellent apartment in the twenty-first century, filled with beautiful, airy things. Of course, he could easily transport himself back, but he could not take Nina with him. He had not yet received permission for that.

The influential personage who transferred him from the seventh to the seventeenth place had somehow guessed that Arden was less in need of an apartment than others.

"After all, you have a place to live," he said when Cloudin was finally admitted to his office after a three-hour wait.

"Oh, but it is very far," said Arden.

"What do you mean, far? Subways and street-car lines will soon be extended to the area."

"No, not to that area."

"They will. The plan has been approved."

"Hardly. My apartment is not here, it's in the twenty-first century."

The influential personage had no capacity for wonder. He had lacked it even as a child.

"I see," he said. "You've turned over your apartment to relatives, and then you come here asking for another. We cannot help you."

And that was the end of the conversation.

The window of Nina's room looked out on an empty lot. One day Nina went to the window, and instead of the empty lot she saw a garden. She guessed it was Arden's doing—he was out at the time. He had turned himself into a garden and was standing under her window, raising to her its strong, firm branches that smelled of late spring.

Then the garden disappeared. Again, there was nothing outside but the empty lot with the dreary booth where a dreary man collected used bottles. Arden must have gotten tired of standing under the window.

She heard his steps on the staircase. But what was known to Nina was not known to the other tenants of the tall building on the corner of Sirius Street and Cosmonaut Avenue. They were delighted to see a garden in place of the lot, and decided that the Park Department, in its concern about beautifying the city, had planted a garden for their benefit. But when the garden disappeared after several hours, they were both astonished and outraged. They felt it was unnatural and illegal, and wanted to submit a collective complaint to the district authorities. However, a little old man, who was retired on pension and who possessed great practical experience and a reasoning mind, proved to them that the phenomenon was quite legitimate.

"It was a movie set," he said.

"And where did it disappear?"

"They took it away."

"Why?"

"They used it for shooting the necessary scene, and then removed it, for the sake of economy. The trees weren't real. Anybody could see that."

Nina begged Cloudin to turn into a garden only at night, when everybody was asleep. He agreed, but rather reluctantly. At night he wanted to sleep, not stand outside the window in the dark.

Their life was much like the lives of other young couples. They missed one another when they parted even for an hour, they lunched and dined together at a little restaurant known by the poetic name of "Ship's Deck" and actually reminiscent of a ship, sailing into the unknown. They were like all newly married couples, with a single, but important, difference. Arden had a strange habit. People usually recall the past, but he recalled the future.

Nina listened with eager interest to stories of how people lived in the century that was still to come. Arden described the future as if it had already happened, and told about it in great detail.

"Were you really there?" Nina sometimes asked doubtingly.

"I was," he answered quietly.

"But why do you speak of it with such sadness? You want to be there again? Are you sorry you are with me, in my time? You want to return? Have you forgotten the road back?"

"Your question is wrong. It is illogical. There are no roads to where I came from."

"Do explain it, Arden."

"For the time being, it is still unexplainable."

[SIX]

The sociologist visited them often with a briefcase bulging with papers. He looked worried. He brought many questionnaires, each one with many questions. He was engaged in a study of the psychology of art and of artists, and he tried to trick Arden into revealing the essence of the creative process.

"You insist," he asked Arden, "that you sometimes have hallucinations, and at such moments it seems to you that you are a garden?"

"It does not seem to me. I really can transform myself. Not always, but most of the time."

"Can you describe your state of mind?"

"I can."

"Please try to be as precise as possible," said the sociologist in the tone of a doctor speaking to a patient.

"I come out into the lot under the window and begin to turn into a garden. I try to do it instantly, so that nobody will notice a man turning into trees. I usually succeed, but not always. The other day the janitress caught me at it and started screaming, 'Just look, look what that crazy man is doing!' A crowd assembled, they were terribly indignant. But an old man saved the situation. 'Can't you see,' he said. 'It's very simple. They're making a movie. He's an actor, playing a part in a fairy tale. They'll finish shooting, and everything will return to normal.' "

"No, this isn't what I mean," the sociologist interrupted. "You are describing the reactions of other people. I am not concerned with that at the moment. I want to know what you feel. Try to describe your own psychological state."

"My psychological state," said Cloudin, "is like a poem. I feel that the world and myself are one. As in a good poem, where there are no logical barriers between phenomena, and the inner life flows freely, like a river."

"And you create at such times?" asked the sociologist.

"It wouldn't really be exact to say that I create—I am moved by something far more powerful than I am."

"You evade my question. Be more specific. What do you feel?"

"I feel like a garden. Trees stand tens, sometimes hundreds of years. I doubt that they would like to change their poses, to sit down, or lie down. They stand. I also stand. But, unlike them, I can leave. The knowledge that I am not bound to the soil also plays a part."

"We don't seem to understand each other," the sociologist said irritably. He sighed, wrote down some notes, and closed his notebook.

[SEVEN]

Only a year passed. But important changes took place in the lives of Arden and Nina. To begin with, he ceased turning into a garden. Gradually he got out of the habit, and then forgot how to do it. His recollections shifted to the past and became like an old family album. His paintings and watercolors no longer charmed Nina with their extraordinary freshness. There was no longer any demand for them at the gallery.

Nina felt sad when the director of the gallery said to her, "Your husband's paintings are just an ordinary drop in a sea of mediocre works."

When she came home, Cloudin was peacefully asleep. Quietly, not to wake him, she collected some used bottles and took them in a shopping bag to the booth in the empty lot.

The old man sat on a bench with an old lady who was proud because she had once been a great beauty. They were warming themselves in the sun.

The former beauty said to the old man:

"An empty lot. And such an ugly one. If they would only plant some trees or flowers. I've been dreaming of it for years."

"What would be the good of it?" the old man answered. "We wouldn't live long enough to see the grown trees. Takes too much time."

Nina was saddened again when she heard the old man's words. She felt sorry for him. Or perhaps she felt sorry for herself, because her life with Arden, which began so magically, had now become so dull.

When she returned to her room, Arden Nikolayevich was already up and getting ready to work. He had long been working on a painting of student sorcerers learning how to perform wonders. But the sorcerers in the painting looked very ordinary, and for some reason they resembled the gloomy man who collected empty bottles.

Nina asked timidly:

"Arden, why do your sorcerers look like the man who has just refused to take two bottles from me?"

She hoped that he would say, "You are posing the question incorrectly." But Cloudin answered, yawning:

"I've forgotten how to work without models. I don't trust imagination. Imagination can lead us away from real life and take us heaven knows where."

"But these are sorcerers!"

"Well, what about it? And what's the good of sorcerers, anyway? That man in the booth is doing an important and useful job—he collects empty bottles."

Arden's words seemed logical enough, and Nina did not know how to answer him.

"Arden," she asked quietly after a while. "Couldn't you turn into a garden again, just for half an hour?"

"What for?"

"I'd like it very much."

"Nonsense. Empty games. In fact, I'm not so sure it is ethical to have such wishes."

Nina waited while he washed his brush and put it down to dry on the window sill. Then they went to lunch at Ship's Deck.

The restaurant no longer resembled a ship, and it did not sail anywhere, but stood in one place, as a restaurant should.

"Arden," Nina asked. "Did you go to the passport office?"

"I did," he answered in a bored voice.

"What for?"

"What do you mean, what for? How can I go around with a passport that says I was born in the year 2003? According to my document, I don't even exist yet. Where's the logic?"

"But I liked it so much, Arden, that you were born in a century that is yet to come. And I was so happy that you could turn into a garden."

"It was ridiculous, Nina. Absurd!"

"I don't know. But when you used to turn into a garden you were different, and your paintings were different. You're like another man now."

[EIGHT]

This time the sociologist came without his briefcase and without questionnaires. He was very upset.

"Arden Nikolayevich," he said with unconcealed anxiety. "Your wife told me the other day that you have stopped turning into a garden."

"I have."

"Why?"

"My turning or non-turning into a garden has nothing to do with causality. It is alogical, in the very nature of the fact. It cannot be explained from the scientific positions of your time."

"But you are repeating the words I spoke to you when I was studying your psychology."

"What of it? I took your advice. And everyone else's. And began to behave in normal, ordinary ways, like all people. I don't understand why you're displeased."

"Couldn't you turn into a garden just once more, just for ten minutes? I beg you, please. I was careless enough to publish a scientific article about your strange ability, and a commission of scholars was appointed to verify my experiment."

"Your experiment?"

"Well, not mine, yours. Or, rather, your capacity to assume another shape. This evening the commission will visit you to study your phenomenal gift."

"I've forgotten how to do it. I'm out of practice. I may not succeed without training."

"Then why not train now? I'll time you."

The sociologist glanced at his watch.

Cloudin walked lazily down to the empty lot. Suddenly, it turned dark. The branches of the garden covering the ground shut out the sky. The fragrance of lilacs and moist greenery wafted into the room.

"Splendid!" said the sociologist to Nina. "It worked! He did it! A truly extraordinary phenomenon. Too bad I don't know how to explain it theoretically. Let us go down and take a walk under the trees. We'll get some fresh air and try to think of a rational theory to account for this incredible fact of spiritual and physical transformation."

Nina and the sociologist went down, crossed the yard, and entered the garden.

The former beauty and the old man were again sitting on a bench. The former beauty said approvingly:

"Look how fast they've learned to grow trees! In the morning there was an empty lot, and now—what a dense, lovely garden!"

"It isn't real," said the old man. "Just a movie set. They'll come and shoot the scene, and then they will remove it. You've got to understand such things."

Nina waited all day, then all night, and all morning. Then twilight came, and then another day, but the garden still stood in the lot.

DMITRY BILENKIN

The Air of Mars

He walked across the cold, red plain for two days and two nights—forward, only forward. He wore a clearly visible bright blue space suit, but he did not delude himself with the hope that he would be found by his comrades. It would be a sheer miracle if the hum of a motor broke into the monotonous howl of Martian air.

He walked like an automaton, in regular, measured steps, saving his energy. Six kilometers an hour, not more and not less. His thoughts were also governed by the rhythm of his steps. Only fragments of what he had seen remained in his memory. The rest flowed together like trailing mist, and all his former life receded somewhere into infinite distance, became small and unreal—a landscape seen through the wrong end of binoculars.

Nor was there any fear. There was only a dull striving forward, dull fatigue in the body, and a dull, blunted mind. The only thing he felt was an increasing pain in his left shoulder, weighted down by the oxygen tank (the tank he had carried on the right had already been used up and discarded). Otherwise, all was in order: he was neither hungry nor thirsty, the electric heating system functioned perfectly, his shoes did not irritate or pinch his feet. He did not have to struggle with the gradual weakening of the body, deprived of the inflow of vital energy; he did not have to crawl, straining the last remnants of his strength, no longer obeying reason but moved solely by instinct. No, even now technology freed him of suffering.

Again and again he mechanically adjusted the oxygen tank to ease the pressure on his shoulder. Whenever he did it, the position of his head changed, and the howling of the wind in his ears (or, rather, in the earphones of his helmet) now increased, now fell. Though it was evening, the air was clear and transparent; the near horizon was etched distinctly across space; the violet sky and the soil were touched by frost, which made the infrequent stars above shine with a stern, steady light.

He still enjoyed crossing the low hills. They sloped gently, so that he did not have to slow his pace, and on the way down he walked faster, glad that the hills increased his speed, although this was an obvious self-deception and he knew it. As a child, he had often imagined that he was not walking, but riding, that he was himself a car, with four wheels instead of two feet. He liked to "step on the gas" and move faster, to "turn the steering wheel" to avoid collision with passersby, and to "step on the brakes." Now he also felt like a machine.

His shadow gradually lengthened. The lower the sun, the more intense became the redness of the plain. The slopes of the hills were aflame, but twilight gathered in the hollows. It lurked there like the velvet paws of some strange savage beast. The wind seemed imperceptibly to die down. Everything stood still, and Severgin (this had been his name once, but now it didn't matter) was chilled within by the anxiety that precedes the coming of night, when man is alone and defenseless in the desert.

He glanced at the sun, and his heart sank. So he had still clung to a deeply buried hope that he'd be rescued. . . . The end of the bright day meant the end of hope.

From far away, from the bluish, undulating hills, something living rolled down; it crossed the shadows and approached Severgin. The little animal's eyes flashed pink, their glance piercing the man. Severgin put his hand on his gun. But the animal did not linger. Recognizing the man as an alien presence, it ran off on its own business. Some wise instinct evidently told the animal that the two-legged creature had nothing to do with Mars, that it was there by chance, that it was alive by chance and would disappear before the sun lit up the plain once more.

Severgin was tempted for an instant to fire at the animal as it ran. He felt a sudden surge of pity for himself. It was as if someone had turned the binoculars and the past had come alive. The past that had predetermined everything. Why was it that nature had made him different from others? Why, why?

Bowing his head, beside himself, he rushed toward the stealthy shadows. Immediately, as he expected, his muscles seemed to fill with lead, but he drove and drove himself on, as though punishing his body.

After a hundred meters he gave up. Any other man of his age and health would easily have run a thousand. But a hundred meters were enough to exhaust him.

It had always been so. He was born defective, not like everybody else. The problem was not something simple, like an allergy to bread, for example. Thousands of people had allergies to one thing or another, and it was nothing but an inconvenience. He had been deprived by nature of something much more important. He was not sicklier than any other children, but he dropped out, breathless, in the hundred-meter race, he could not pull himself up on the bars, he cried trying to shinny up a pole or scale the wall on a rope ladder.

No, he was capable of prolonged physical activity such as walking long distances. The trouble lay elsewhere. There seemed to be a kind of built-in damper in his organism. He was as incapable of sharp effort, requiring a quick spurt of energy, as a turned-down wick is incapable of producing a bright flame.

The other boys treated him with tolerant condescension, as a weakling, and the gym teachers detested him. The doctors had diagnosed the boy as "healthy." He had a normal body and normal limbs. What right had he to frustrate and humiliate them, hanging on the rope like a sack of potatoes? Gym classes were the nightmare of Severgin's childhood and adolescence. At the sight of bars or rings he shook like someone condemned to torture. "Hey, champion!" the kids teased him in the dusty gym that reeked of sweat. And he'd go numb in advance, anticipating the laughter (good-natured, but still insulting) that would greet his clumsy, ignominious attempt to leap across the horse.

He was finally spared this misery by the fourth or fifth doctor to whom his alarmed parents had taken him. This doctor, like the others, found nothing wrong with his heart or lungs, but he didn't shrug his shoulders or treat the boy as a malingerer. Instead, he calmly said, "Metabolic deviation, evidently genetic. For the time being, incurable. But don't let it worry you. You won't be a football player. As for the rest. . . . You'll do all right. If you had lived in the days of the cave men, you'd have been eaten by the first tiger, but what does it matter today? Just pay no attention to it."

The nightmare was laid to rest. But evidently not entirely.

And this was what it had led to in the end—a deserted Martian plain in the dying light, a frenzied effort to escape from his own self. . . .

Severgin compelled himself to lie down, resting his raised feet on a knoll to give them a chance to relax. The simple movements calmed him. The burst of despair restored him to sanity.

It was his own fault; he had no one to blame. He had challenged fate in going to Mars. Not, of course, as in boyhood, when, crying with rage, he had driven himself to effort after effort, either to win or to drop breathless. These efforts had long been abandoned by Dr. Severgin, eminent microbiologist. He had long lived in a world where everything was determined by the mind, and physical endowments played no part. In that world he was in his right place—indeed, more than in his right place. And no wonder it was he, rather than someone else, who had been asked to make an emergency flight to Mars in order to examine the troubling behavior of the crystallobacteria that had inexplicably penetrated the filters of the water-purifying system. No one cared whether he could or could not raise himself on parallel bars. Mars needed his mind, not his muscles.

He could have refused to go, but he didn't. To be selected for the journey to Mars, to approach the very farthest frontier where man waged a stern battle for survival—how could he reject such brilliant compensation for all the humiliations of his childhood? He was elated. Besides, no one demanded that he enter into hand-to-hand combat with nature. On Mars, as on earth, he would remain a passenger on the ship called civilization, shielded from all storms by trusty portholes.

No one thought of the possibility of catastrophe. Does a captain ever ask his passengers whether they know how to swim?

On the last lap of his journey, he flew from the space station to Mars seated comfortably in the tiny automatic rocket which rose by itself, landed by itself, and did everything by itself. He sat in the armchair, reading, when suddenly he looked up and saw rocky ground rapidly approaching from below. He had not noticed, and now nobody would ever know, what had gone wrong in the mechanism. But even as it fell, the rocket took care of him: he was catapulted out before he had time to realize what was happening.

There was only one thing the machine could not do—protect him from hitting a rock as he parachuted down. Fortunately, the blow was softened by Severgin's pouch of emergency rations; he himself was not hurt. Part of the rations turned into a mess, silvered with fragments of the coffee thermos, but everything else was safe, including his precious map that made it possible for him to establish his exact location wherever he might be.

He took his bearings the moment he came to. Everything was all right—and all wrong. He was in the southern region of the Mitchell range, outside the path set for the rocket and outside the zone of radar observation. This meant that the space station could not have recorded the place of his crash even approximately. On the other hand, he was only about 160 kilometers from the geologists' camp. The oxygen supply in his space suit and the emergency reserves would last thirty-six hours. He also had enough tablets to keep him awake. The mountainous terrain ended about seven kilometers from the site of the crash, and the mountains were neither too steep nor too high. It should take six hours or so to cross the mountains, and beyond them was the plain where it would not be difficult to maintain a steady speed of approximately five and a half kilometers an hour. He'd make it to the camp. After all, walking wasn't running; his organism wouldn't let him down.

For a fleeting moment he even welcomed the accident—an unexpected chance to redeem his childhood failures. He smiled: so they still rankled despite all he had achieved! He sprayed the crash site with fluorescent paint and set out at a brisk pace.

He had not reckoned, however, with the fact that even low mountains required some climbing, jumping across crevasses, heaving oneself up occasional rocky cliffs; in other words, doing all the things he was incapable of. Instead of proceeding directly, he had to circle obstacles. Instead of the six, or, at most, eight hours it would have taken a normal man to cross the mountains, it took him fifteen hours.

He went on, already realizing that he would run out of oxygen long before he could get to the camp. . . .

The little Martian sun touched the edge of the plain. Severgin stood up. His shadow, grown longer now, leaped toward the horizon. He had to go on, so that the very rhythm of walking would lull his aroused emotions.

Before he reached the end of the first kilometer, the plain darkened. But in the sky above, small fleecy clouds, invisible by daylight, lit up one after the other, as if someone were touching them, picking out chords of light-music. Golden, lilac, red—the tones were delicate, airy, high, floating in the violet crystal of the sky like petals of transparent flowers.

Severgin raised his head and walked, smiling at something, astonished at his own smile, and wishing to remain forever as he was at this moment.

Man should not argue with nature—he understood that now. He should not demand that it provide him with comfortable pillows, but accept whatever it gave and love every instant of life because, whatever happened, death was waiting in the end. What if life did not entirely satisfy one's expectations? A stone falls, a river flows, man seeks happiness. Everything proceeds according to its own laws; they must be understood—and argument is futile.

Imperceptibly Severgin crossed that boundary which divides the period of life undarkened by approaching death from the final stage, when the end is known and near. Different people cross this boundary in different ways, but all discover beyond it something new to them—something awesome, great, containing both terror and reconciliation.

The sky turned black, but the darkness did not last. Deimos rose, silvering the ground, and the chill that gripped Severgin's knees at every step, when the fabric of his suit tightened over them, grew sharper. He turned up the electric heating system.

The plain was flat now, spreading before him like a smooth sheet, but here and there a narrow strip of shadow lay across it, thrown by the infrequent blades of safar—the dreary Martian grass. Severgin suddenly became aware that he avoided stepping on it, and wondered where the instinct to spare it had come from.

Then he remembered. Once, on a dull and windy April day, he had walked in a forest of oak trees. The trees still held their winter bareness, gnarled and dark; the earth was covered with brittle leaves, and acorns, brown-gray like the leaves, crunched underfoot. It was pleasant to hear this crunching. The sound reflected the strength of a man who was sure of himself, the weight of his strong, healthy body. And so he walked on till his eye was caught by a pale-green star amidst the wilted grass. He bent down, wondering, and saw an acorn seedling already gripping the cold earth with its new root. And then he saw that there were many little stars around him, that they were everywhere, and that he had been crushing them as he walked. He hastened to get out of the wood on tiptoe.

Severgin halted, as he had at that time, and bent down over a safar blade. For some reason, taking a good look at it seemed more important than anything else he might do.

The stem of the safar plant resembled a rusty wire stuck slantwise into the frozen ground. It was stronger than a steel wire, it could not be crushed like an acorn. Severgin knew this. But the safar was also waiting for the hour of its awakening. In this rarefied atmosphere, so poor in oxygen and warmth, it too had its spring. It did not languish; it lived perfectly well in conditions deadly to everything that came from earth and was not protected by space suits or greenhouse walls.

This also was to be accepted.

Suddenly a second shadow fell from the plant, slender as a knitting needle. Phobos, the second moon of Mars, was rising.

Severgin straightened up. He was surrounded by a

brightly lit plain, with narrow double shadows scattered over it like cuneiform characters. Severgin, silvered by the moons, stood like a monument amid the dark ancient writing.

And yet there was life around him. How many times, peering into the sharply outlined field of a microscope, had he admired its persistence! Often the objective looked like a battlefield, densely covered with the corpses of bacteria killed by poisons, ultraviolet rays, radiation. Not a trace of movement—as at this moment. But that was a delusion. One organism in millions, one of billions often survived and gave rise to a new race of mutants. The unknown factor that distinguished it from all the rest triumphed over the circumstances and won a new sphere for life where it seemed that there was nothing to sustain it.

This was how it had always been. No mistake in nature was ever a mistake. Originating in water, terrestrial life conquered dry land, emerged into the air, burrowed down into the depths of the earth. Who knows—perhaps, even without man, its pressure would after millions of years throw out into space the seeds of new harvests, to reach other planets. And why not? Dry land had also been a deadly desert to the denizens of the sea. Yet, drawn by a chain of circumstances, they advanced, wave after wave, and out of the billions that perished there would always emerge some individuals, different from the rest, who managed to survive in new conditions.

But it was only then that their existence justified itself. In ordinary circumstances these divergent individuals were the first to perish. When a flock of birds is caught up in a storm, death does not choose its victims blindly. The average, the standard, developed and tested through millions of years of evolution, withstand the storm precisely because their organism has been perfected through thousands of past storms. But woe to those who deviate from the norm.

Severgin was such a deviant, and therefore the mountains had defeated him. Technology had made it possible for people to suffer few losses in their search for new worlds. But it was subject to occasional failures—otherwise there would have been no losses. Its protective shield, alas, was not and could not be absolute.

Severgin wondered why, of all things he could be thinking of during his final hours, he thought of this. Was he seeking consolation in reason, because the mind could not accept senselessness, either in life or in death? As though this could make dying easier!

Illimitable silence surrounded him. The moons converged and stared intently from above like two eyes. Movement in this frozen world seemed sacrilege. But Severgin walked faster.

No, he would not do it. He would not draw his gun and shoot himself when he began to suffocate. The manner of his death would make a difference to the living. Finding him with a hole in his heart would strike a painful blow at his friends. Was he afraid they would see it as an act of cowardice? No, it wasn't that. Simply, a man must fight to his last breath. As grass does, as bacteria do. The measure of mankind's strength depends on the measure of strength of every individual, that's all.

He walked on, thinking about his friends, about those he loved, about what he had accomplished and had not accomplished. Much of what had once seemed important was now entirely trivial. Fame, power, success. They did not sustain man at the moment of death. Before death and after it, man was alive by the good he had done for others. Only friendship, gratitude, and love could bring support and peace at the moments of the summing up. Especially love.

How differently he would live now if it were not too late! It was too late.

Phobos set. A light pre-dawn breeze stirred the air. So he would last till morning. For some odd reason, he wanted it to happen in the light of the sun.

But now the air regulator clicked three times. He shivered. It was the signal that the oxygen would be exhausted in ten minutes. The end.

His numbed feet led him by themselves to a frost-whitened stone. He sat down. The sky on the horizon paled, but it was still long before sunrise.

Should he switch off the heating system and freeze to death? People said it was like falling asleep.

Then suddenly, he was swept by a violent, animal desire to live, to live at any cost! There was too much he had not finished, had not done, had not rectified. . . . He had not had enough of love! He could not simply vanish, cease to be!

He jumped up. And was breathless. As though a mask were pressed against his lips. Yet still he went on. His lungs rose and fell, faster, faster. They were convulsed with pain. A rattle came from his constricted throat. He dropped down to his knees, but still crawled forward. And when his mind turned blank and his body thrashed about in agony, he tore off his helmet and gulped the Martian wind as a drowning man gulps water, because he cannot help but gulp it.

A chill passed through his lungs, a last intolerable flash of pain, and everything went black.

Everything went black, only to start glimmering again.

He came to slowly from the convulsions that had seemed to tear his lungs apart and saw something wavering and red before his eyes.

With an incredible effort he raised his head. It was already light. And he was crawling! He was breathing Martian air! His organism was different from others—he survived!

He did not even realize this. He did not think. He continued to crawl, fiercely, stubbornly, no longer obeying reason, but moved by pure instinct, on and on, toward the place where there were people.

Notes on the Authors

VLADLEN BAKHNOV, born in 1924, is a graduate of the Gorky Literary Institute in Moscow. A contributor since 1946 to various newspapers and magazines, he is also the author of several books of humorous verse, as well as comedies and motion-picture scripts. "Twelve Holidays" was included in his first collection of science fiction, published in 1970. Both the story and the collection are written in the comic manner characteristic of his work.

DMITRY BILENKIN, born in 1933, is a geologist and geochemist who has written a number of popular scientific books and articles. His science fiction stories, which have appeared since 1964 in many magazines and collections, are often concerned with character and man's confrontation with natural forces, on earth and on other planets.

KIRILL BULYCHEV is a historian by profession. During the past ten years he has written a number of brilliantly imaginative science fiction stories, both serious and humorous.

SEVER GANSOVSKY, born in 1918, worked at many trades before World War II, including those of stevedore, sailor, electrician, mailman, and teacher. Severely wounded in the war, he was demobilized and entered the school of philology at Leningrad University. His first published work appeared in 1950. He began writing science fiction in the 1960s.

GENNADY GOR is an ethnographer whose field is the art and folklore of the peoples of the Russian north. Born in 1907, he spent his first year in prison with his parents, who had been sentenced for revolutionary activity. He began to write in 1925 and has since published more than twenty books of essays and stories, as well as several novels. He has been writing science fiction since 1961.

VICTOR KOLUPAYEV, born in 1936, is a fairly recent arrival on the science fiction scene. "A Ticket to Childhood," his first published science fiction story, appeared in 1969. He has since written many stories of space and time, published in various magazines and collections.

OLGA LARIONOVA, an engineer, was born in 1935. Her first science fiction story was published in 1964. In her warm and elegantly written stories, she is more interested in character, motivation, and relationships between people—and sometimes between people and other-planetary beings—than in the physical sciences.

YEREMEY PARNOV, born in 1935, and MIKHAIL YEMTSEV, born in 1930, are both research scientists working in the fields of physics and chemistry. Authors of scientific works, they began to collaborate on science fiction in 1961. Their stories and novels cover a variety of subjects, from the relatively simple and moving friendship between man and dolphin that we find in "The White Pilot" to witty elaborations on the most advanced of recent scientific theories and discoveries.

VALENTINA ZHURAVLEVA, a doctor by training, was born in 1933. Her earliest science fiction stories were published in 1958. She has since abandoned medicine to become a writer, and has numerous stories and collections to her credit.

MIRRA GINSBURG's superb translations have covered a broad range of Russian literature. Her picture-book stories are popular favorites with children, and she has won recognition as the translator of such celebrated authors as Yevgeny Zamyatin, Mikhail Bulgakov and Isaac Bashevis Singer. She was awarded a Guggenheim Fellowship in 1975–76 to translate works by Alexey Remizov.

She is the translator-editor of two other Soviet science-fiction collections, *The Last Door to Aya* and *The Ultimate Threshold*, and has translated a science-fiction novel, *Daughter of Night* by Lydia Obukhova, and many other books.